THE SPRITE AND THE GARDENER

ONI PRESS

AN ONI PRESS PUBLICATION

THE SPRIT
GAR

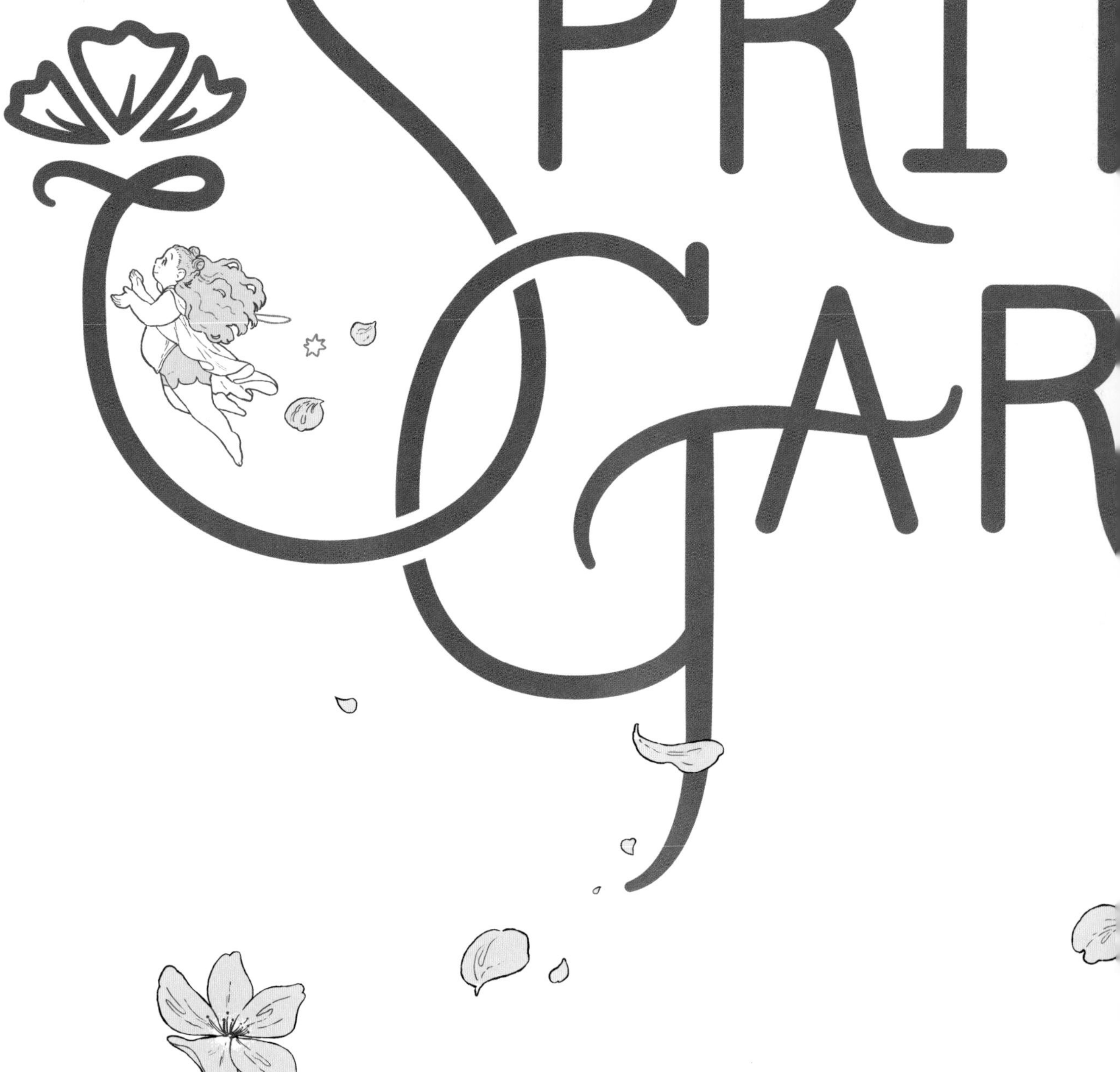

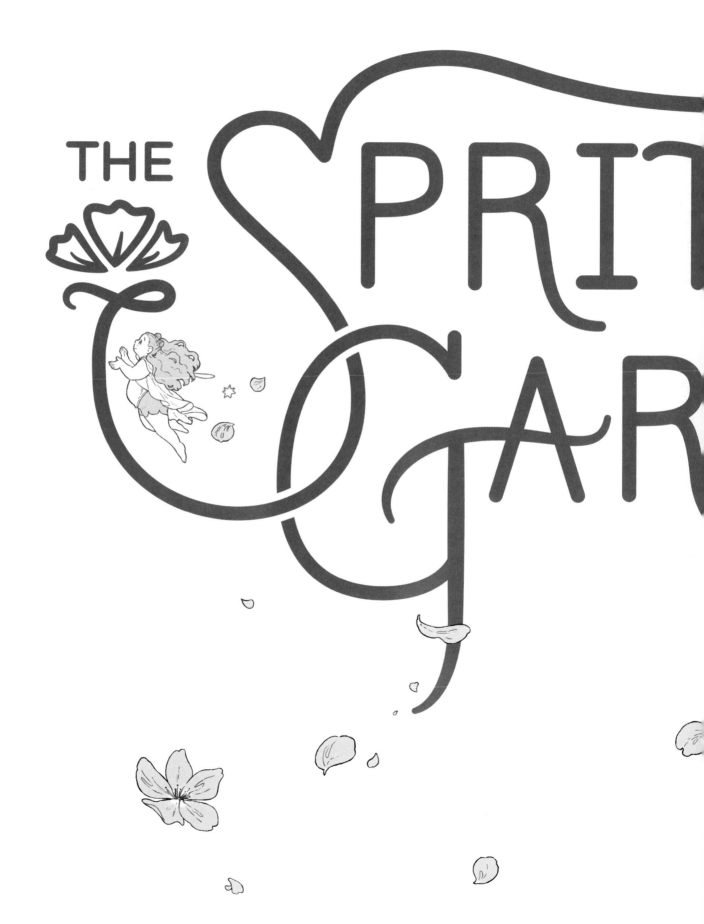

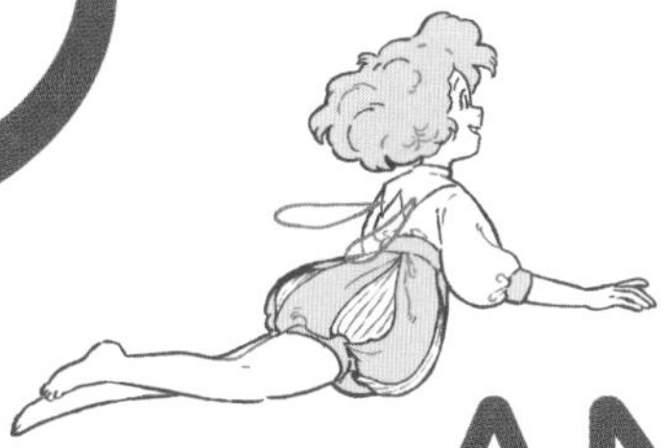

E AND THE

DENER

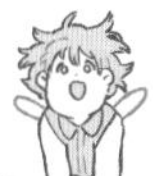

Written by Rii Abrego and Joe Whitt
Illustrated by Rii Abrego
Lettered by Crank!

Designed by Kate Z. Stone
Edited by Ari Yarwood with Robin Herrera and Grace Scheipeter

---

Published by Oni-Lion Forge Publishing Group, LLC

James Lucas Jones, president & publisher • Sarah Gaydos, editor in chief • Charlie Chu, e.v.p. of creative & business development • Brad Rooks, director of operations Amber O'Neill, special projects manager • Margot Wood, director of marketing & sales • Devin Funches, sales & marketing manager • Katie Sainz, marketing manager Tara Lehmann, publicist • Troy Look, director of design & production • Kate Z. Stone, senior graphic designer • Sonja Synak, graphic designer • Hilary Thompson, graphic designer • Sarah Rockwell, graphic designer • Angie Knowles, digital prepress lead Vincent Kukua, digital prepress technician • Jasmine Amiri, senior editor • Shawna Gore, senior editor • Amanda Meadows, senior editor • Robert Meyers, senior editor, licensing • Desiree Rodriguez, editor • Grace Scheipeter, editor • Zack Soto, editor Chris Cerasi, editorial coordinator • Steve Ellis, vice president of games • Ben Eisner, game developer • Michelle Nguyen, executive assistant • Jung Lee, logistics coordinator

Joe Nozemack, publisher emeritus

1319 SE Martin Luther King, Jr. Blvd, Suite 240
Portland, OR 97214

onipress.com   lionforge.com
@onipress   @lionforge

@joeobligations
riiabrego.com | @riibrego
@ccrank

First Edition: May 2021
ISBN: 978-1-62010-906-9
eISBN: 978-1-62010-912-0

Library of Congress Control Number: 2020947306

Printed in China.

1 3 5 7 9 10 8 6 4 2

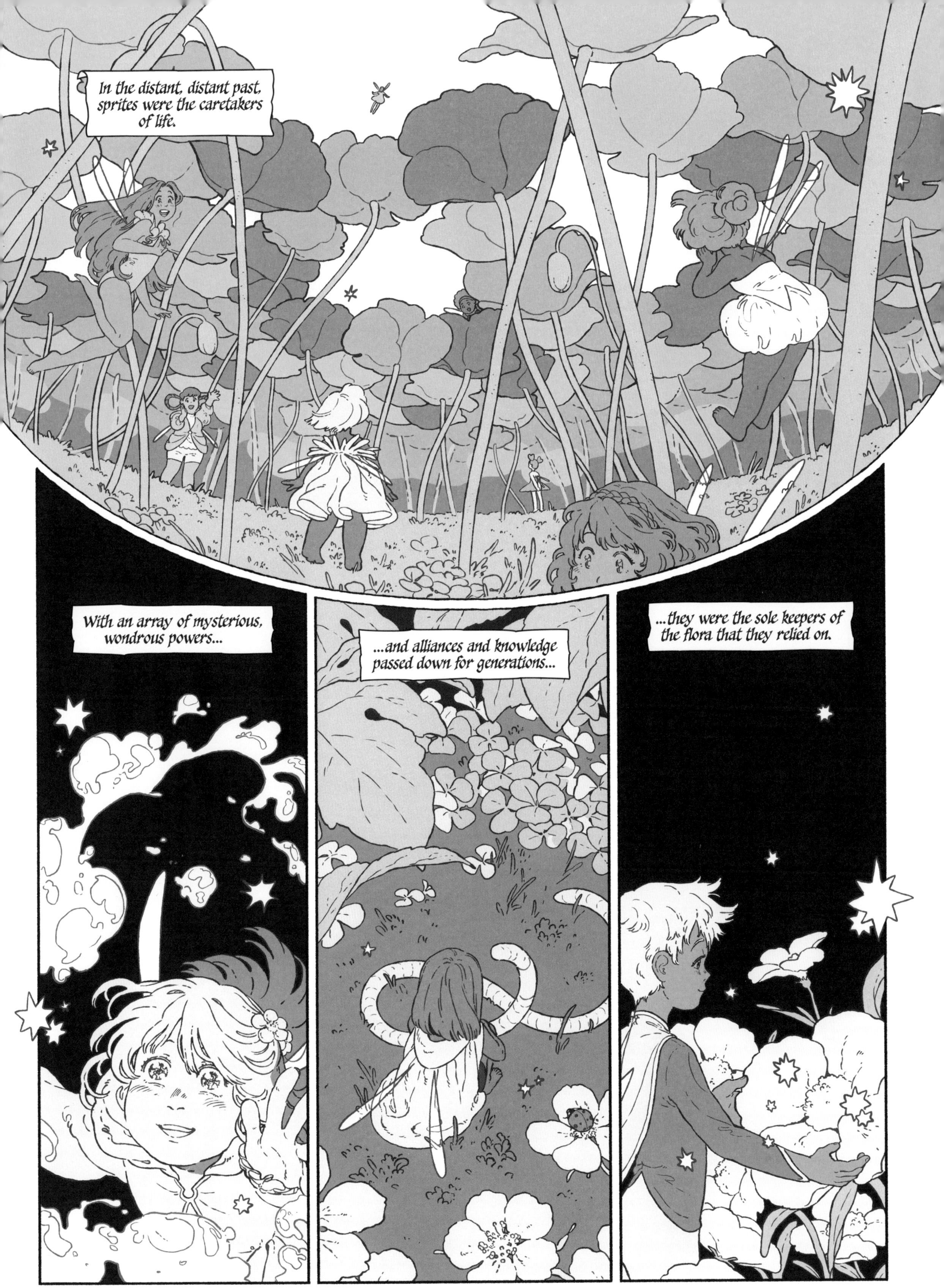
In the distant, distant past, sprites were the caretakers of life.
With an array of mysterious, wondrous powers...
...and alliances and knowledge passed down for generations...
...they were the sole keepers of the flora that they relied on.

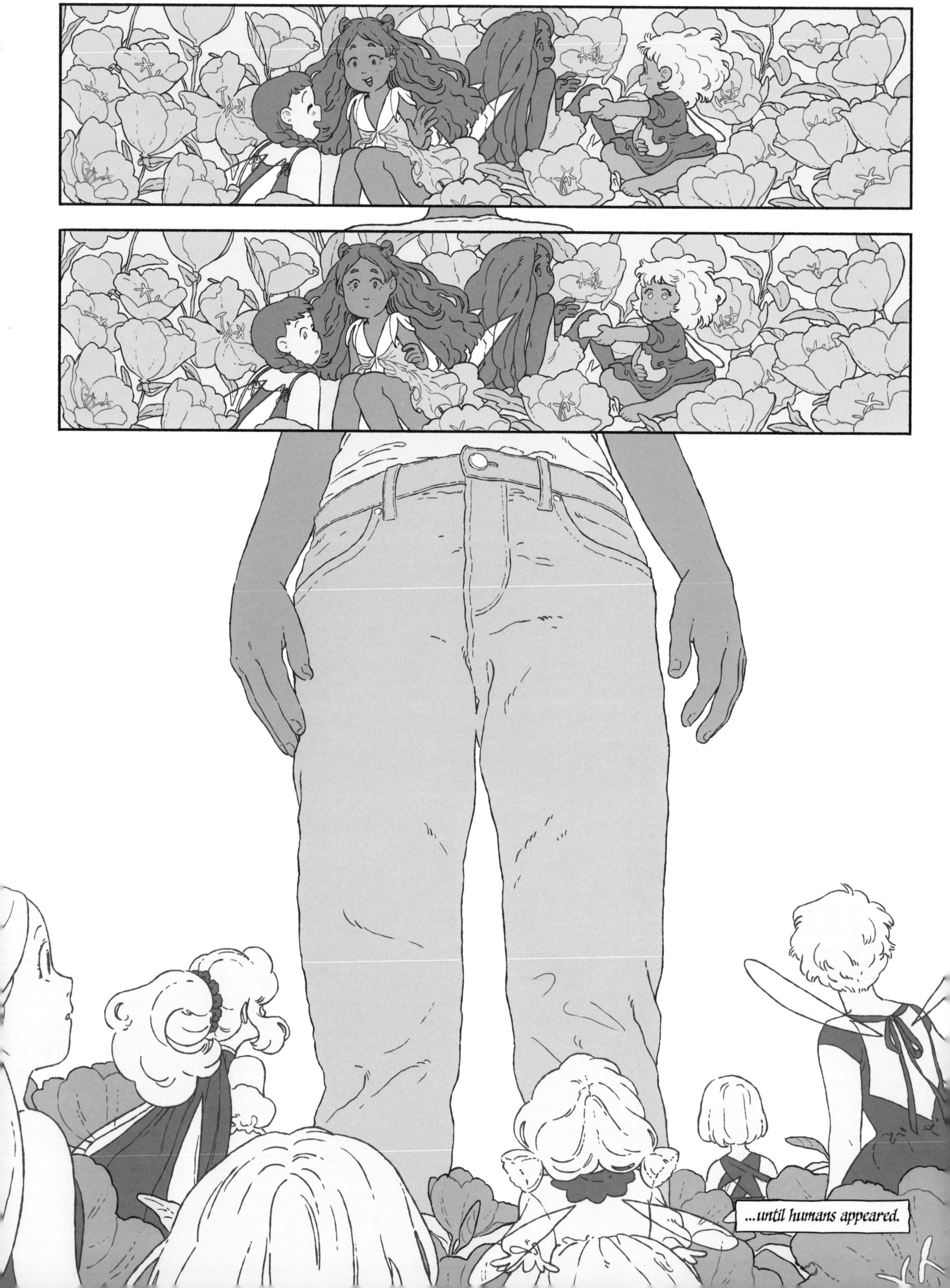
...until humans appeared.

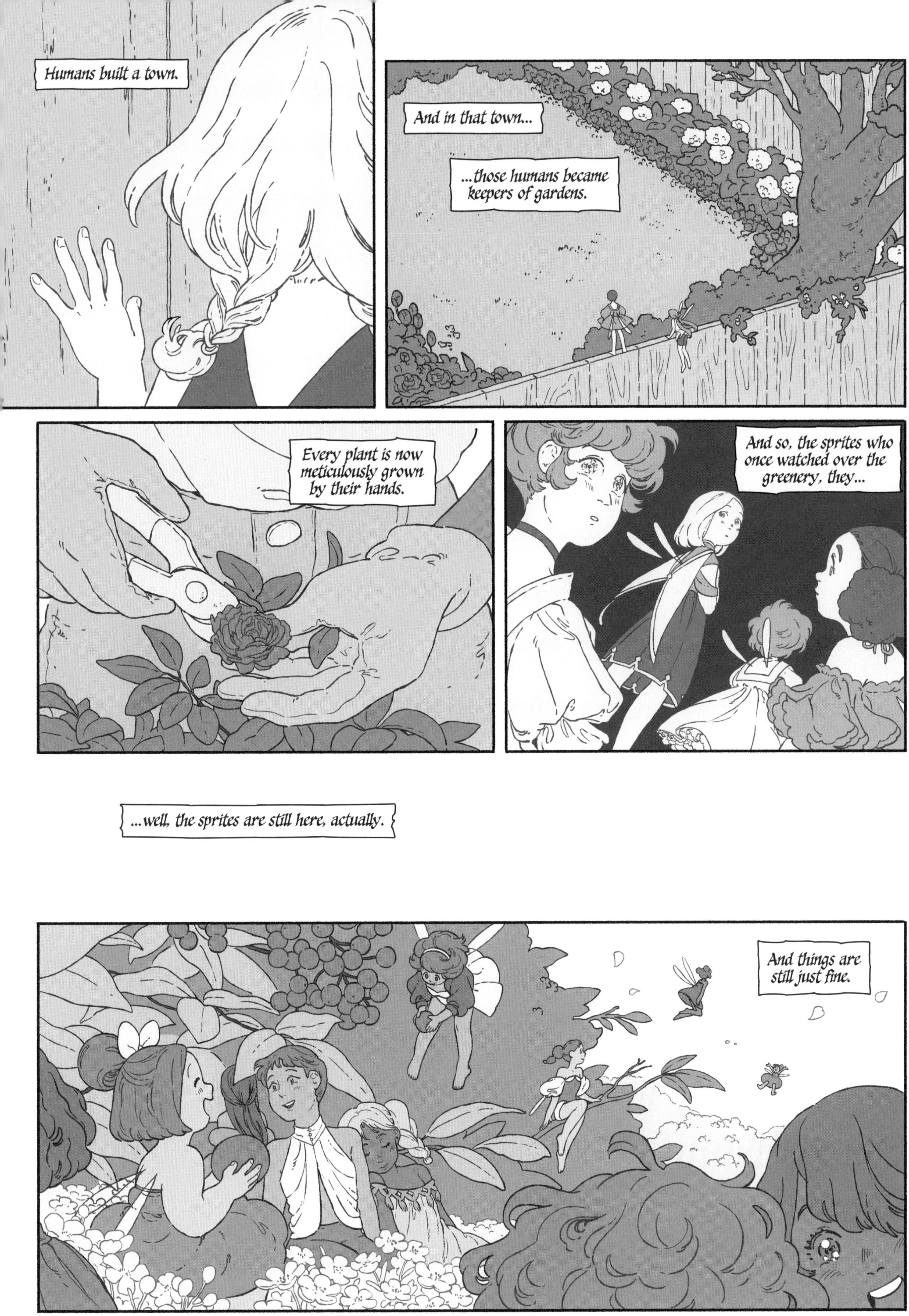
Humans built a town.
And in that town...
...those humans became keepers of gardens.
Every plant is now meticulously grown by their hands.
And so, the sprites who once watched over the greenery, they...
...well, the sprites are still here, actually.
And things are still just fine.

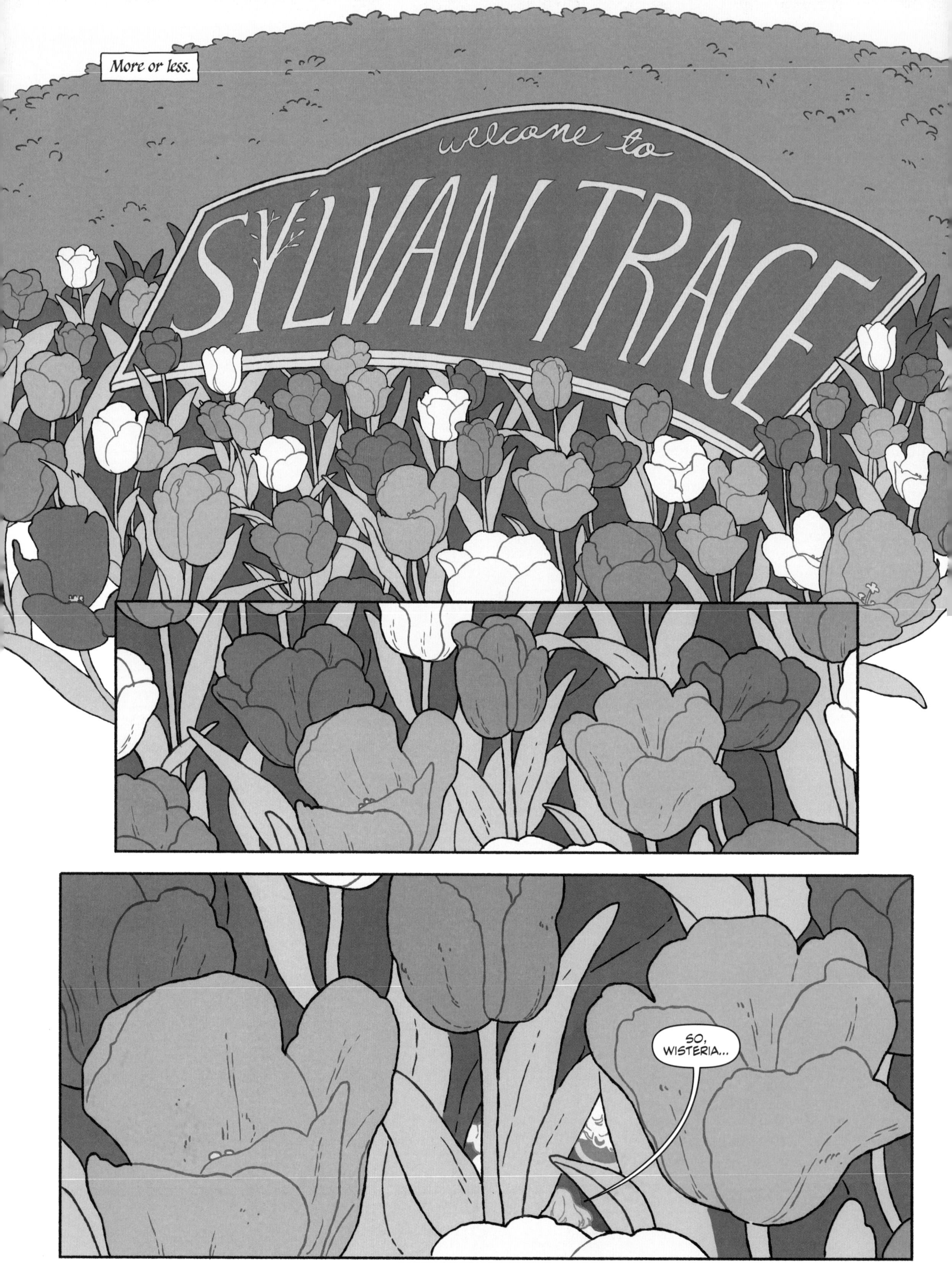
More or less.
welcome to
SYLVAN TRACE
SO, WISTERIA...

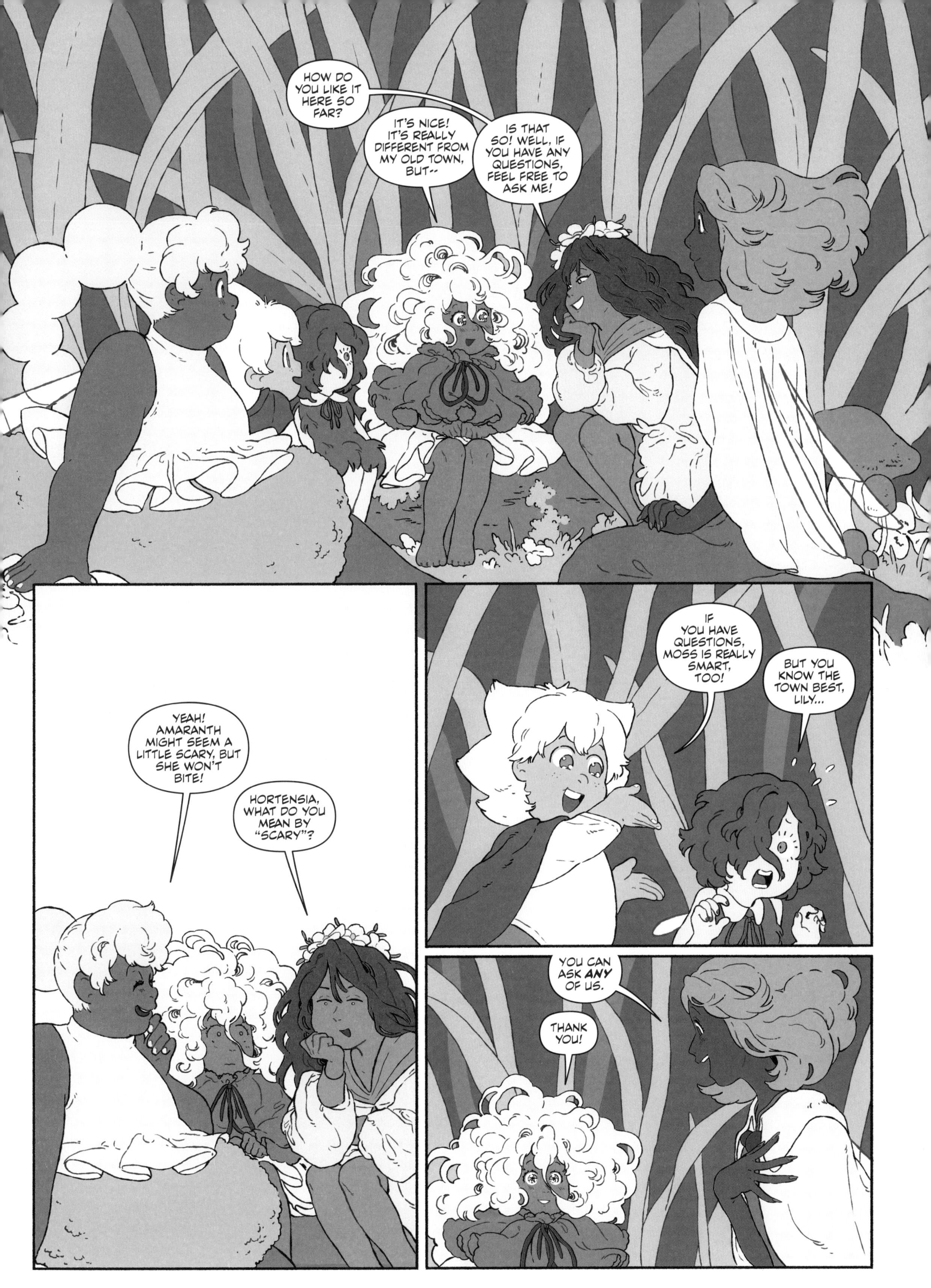
HOW DO YOU LIKE IT HERE SO FAR?
IT'S NICE! IT'S REALLY DIFFERENT FROM MY OLD TOWN, BUT--
IS THAT SO! WELL, IF YOU HAVE ANY QUESTIONS, FEEL FREE TO ASK ME!
YEAH! AMARANTH MIGHT SEEM A LITTLE SCARY, BUT SHE WON'T BITE!
HORTENSIA, WHAT DO YOU MEAN BY "SCARY"?
IF YOU HAVE QUESTIONS, MOSS IS REALLY SMART, TOO!
BUT YOU KNOW THE TOWN BEST, LILY...
YOU CAN ASK ANY OF US.
THANK YOU!

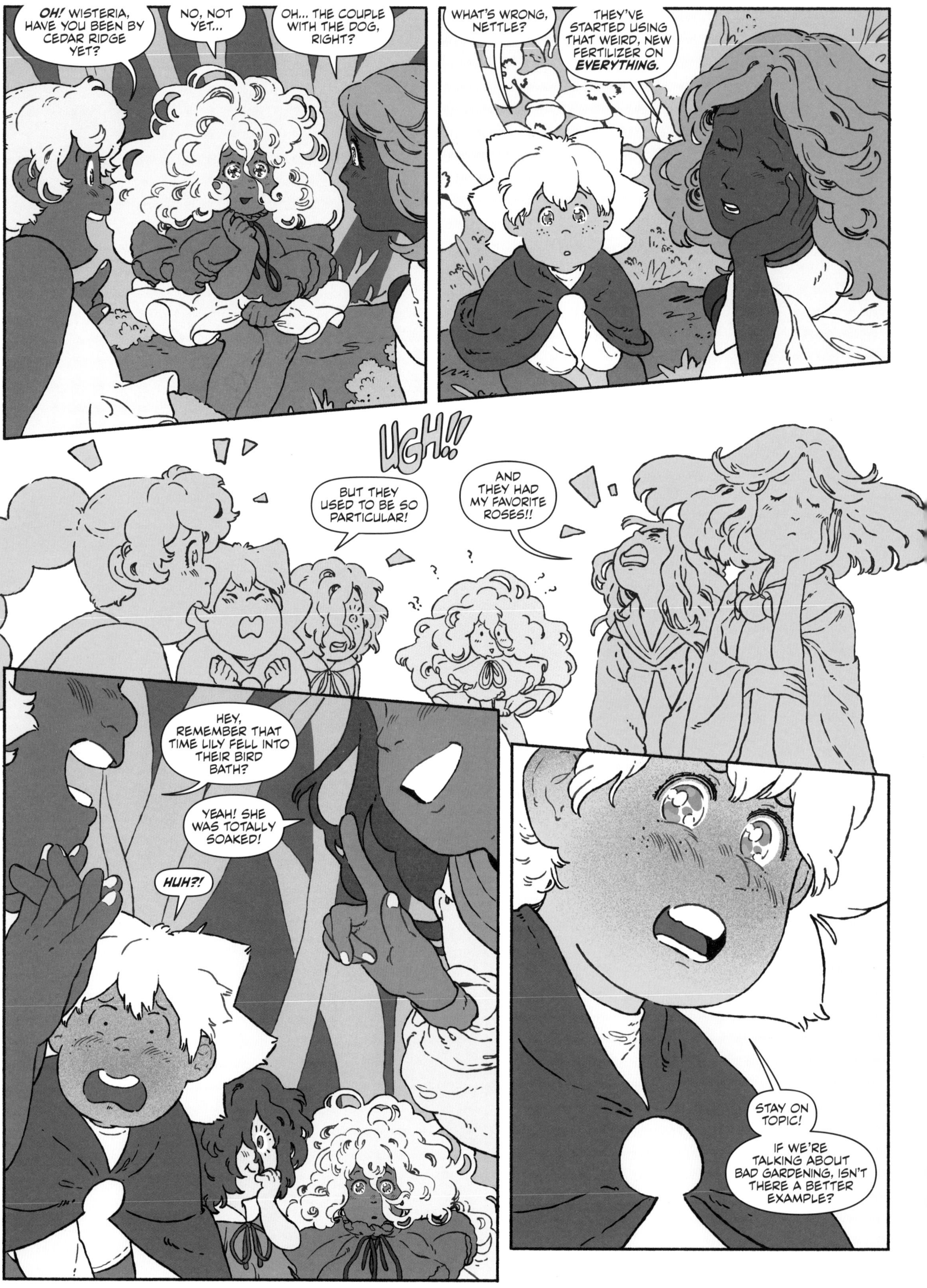

OH! WISTERIA, HAVE YOU BEEN BY CEDAR RIDGE YET?
NO, NOT YET...
OH... THE COUPLE WITH THE DOG, RIGHT?
WHAT'S WRONG, NETTLE?
THEY'VE STARTED USING THAT WEIRD, NEW FERTILIZER ON EVERYTHING.
UGH!!
BUT THEY USED TO BE SO PARTICULAR!
AND THEY HAD MY FAVORITE ROSES!!
HEY, REMEMBER THAT TIME LILY FELL INTO THEIR BIRD BATH?
YEAH! SHE WAS TOTALLY SOAKED!
HUH?!
STAY ON TOPIC!
IF WE'RE TALKING ABOUT BAD GARDENING, ISN'T THERE A BETTER EXAMPLE?

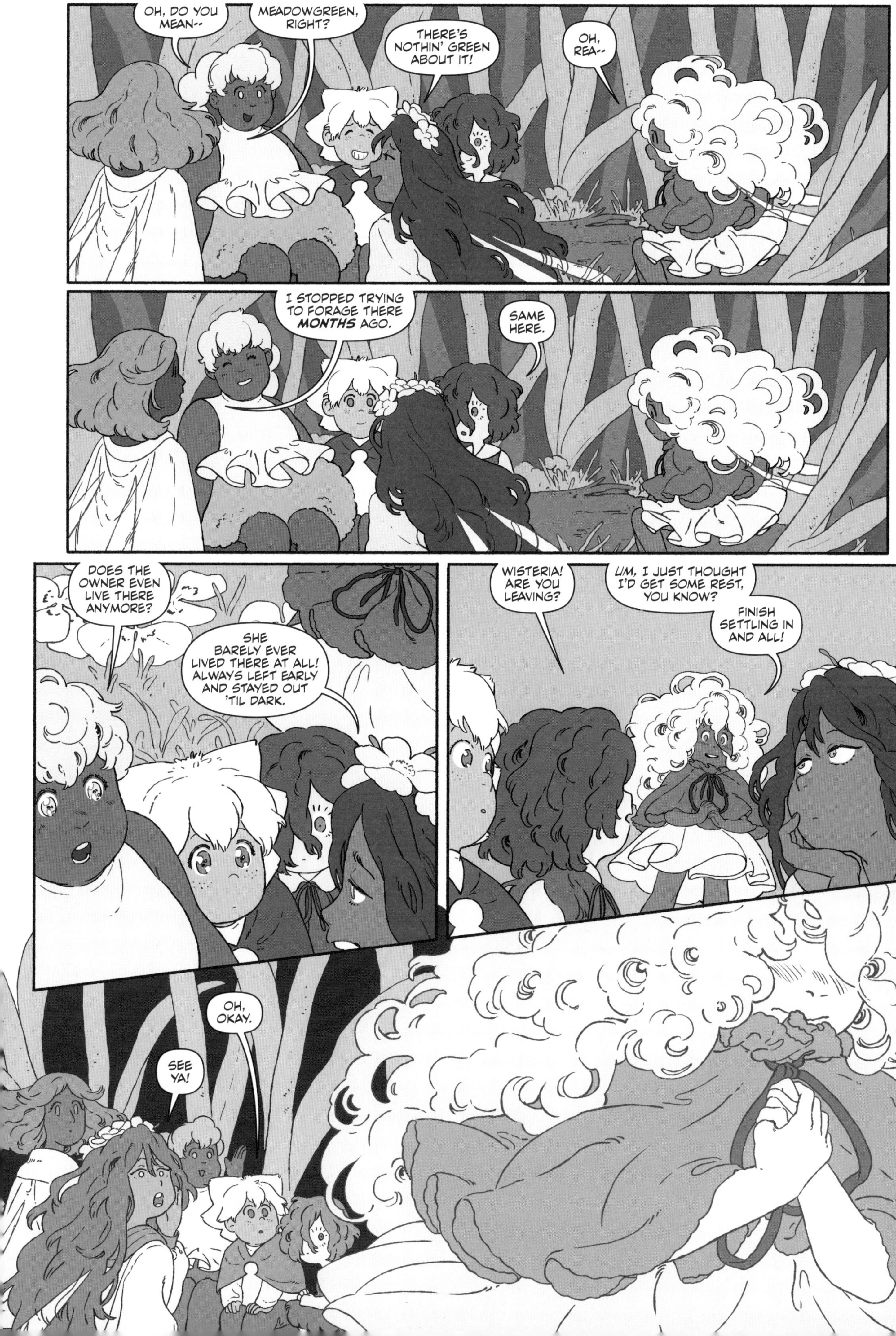
OH, DO YOU MEAN--
MEADOWGREEN, RIGHT?
THERE'S NOTHIN' GREEN ABOUT IT!
OH, REA--
I STOPPED TRYING TO FORAGE THERE MONTHS AGO.
SAME HERE.
DOES THE OWNER EVEN LIVE THERE ANYMORE?
SHE BARELY EVER LIVED THERE AT ALL! ALWAYS LEFT EARLY AND STAYED OUT 'TIL DARK.
WISTERIA! ARE YOU LEAVING?
UM, I JUST THOUGHT I'D GET SOME REST, YOU KNOW?
FINISH SETTLING IN AND ALL!
OH, OKAY.
SEE YA!

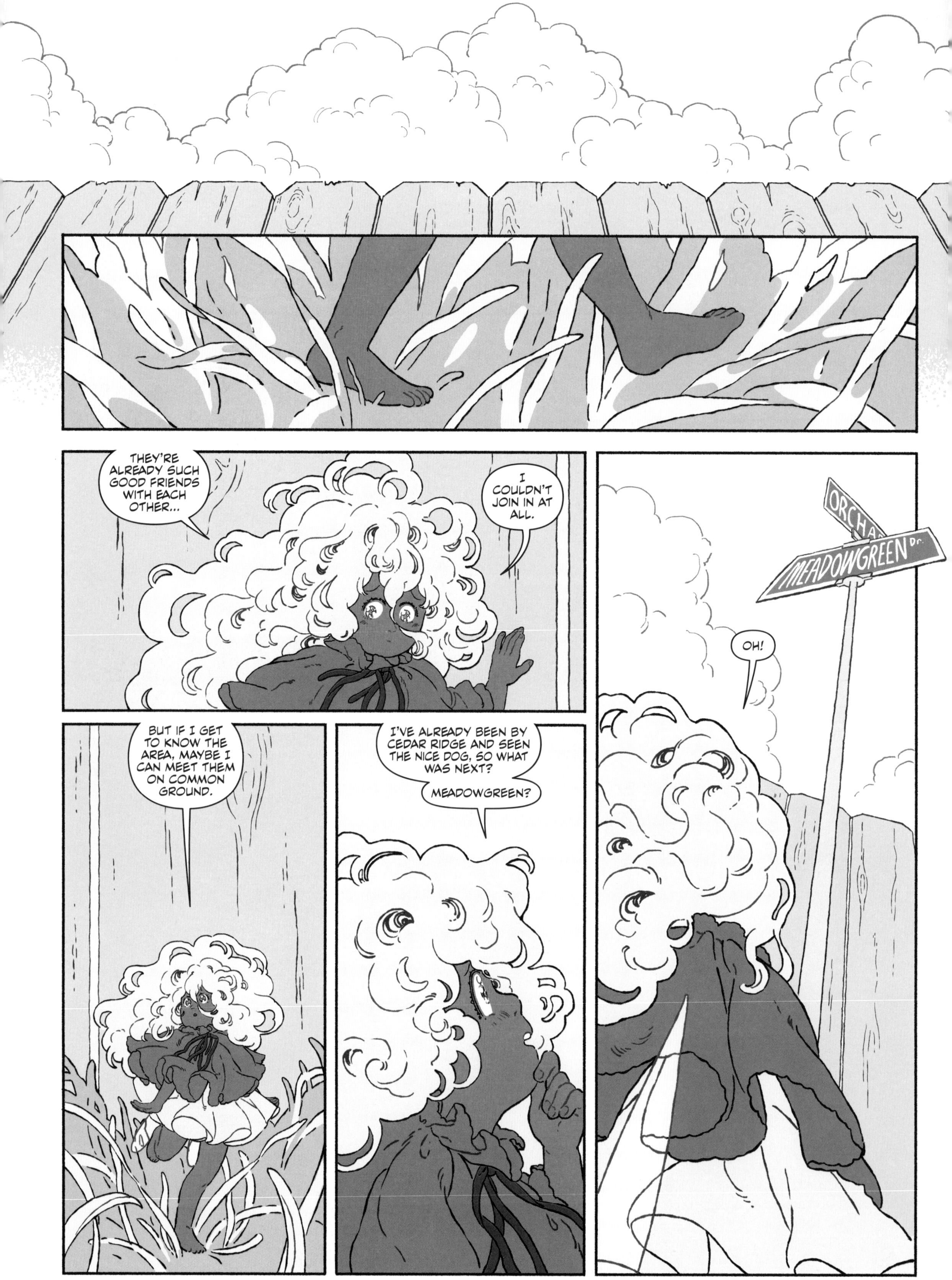
THEY'RE ALREADY SUCH GOOD FRIENDS WITH EACH OTHER...
I COULDN'T JOIN IN AT ALL.
ORCHA
MEADOWGREEN Dr.
OH!
BUT IF I GET TO KNOW THE AREA, MAYBE I CAN MEET THEM ON COMMON GROUND.
I'VE ALREADY BEEN BY CEDAR RIDGE AND SEEN THE NICE DOG, SO WHAT WAS NEXT?
MEADOWGREEN?

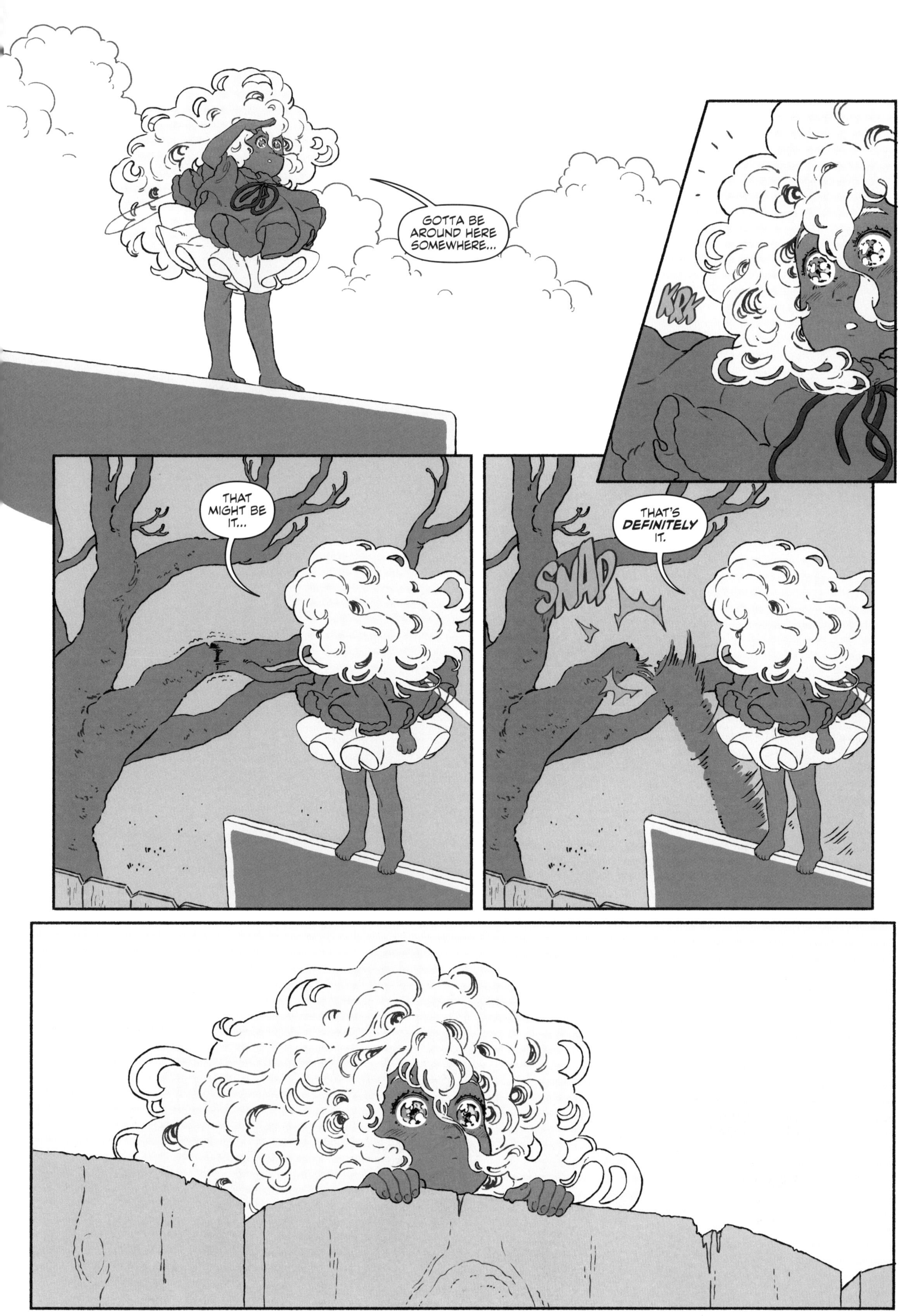
GOTTA BE AROUND HERE SOMEWHERE...
KRK
THAT MIGHT BE IT...
SNAP
THAT'S *DEFINITELY* IT.

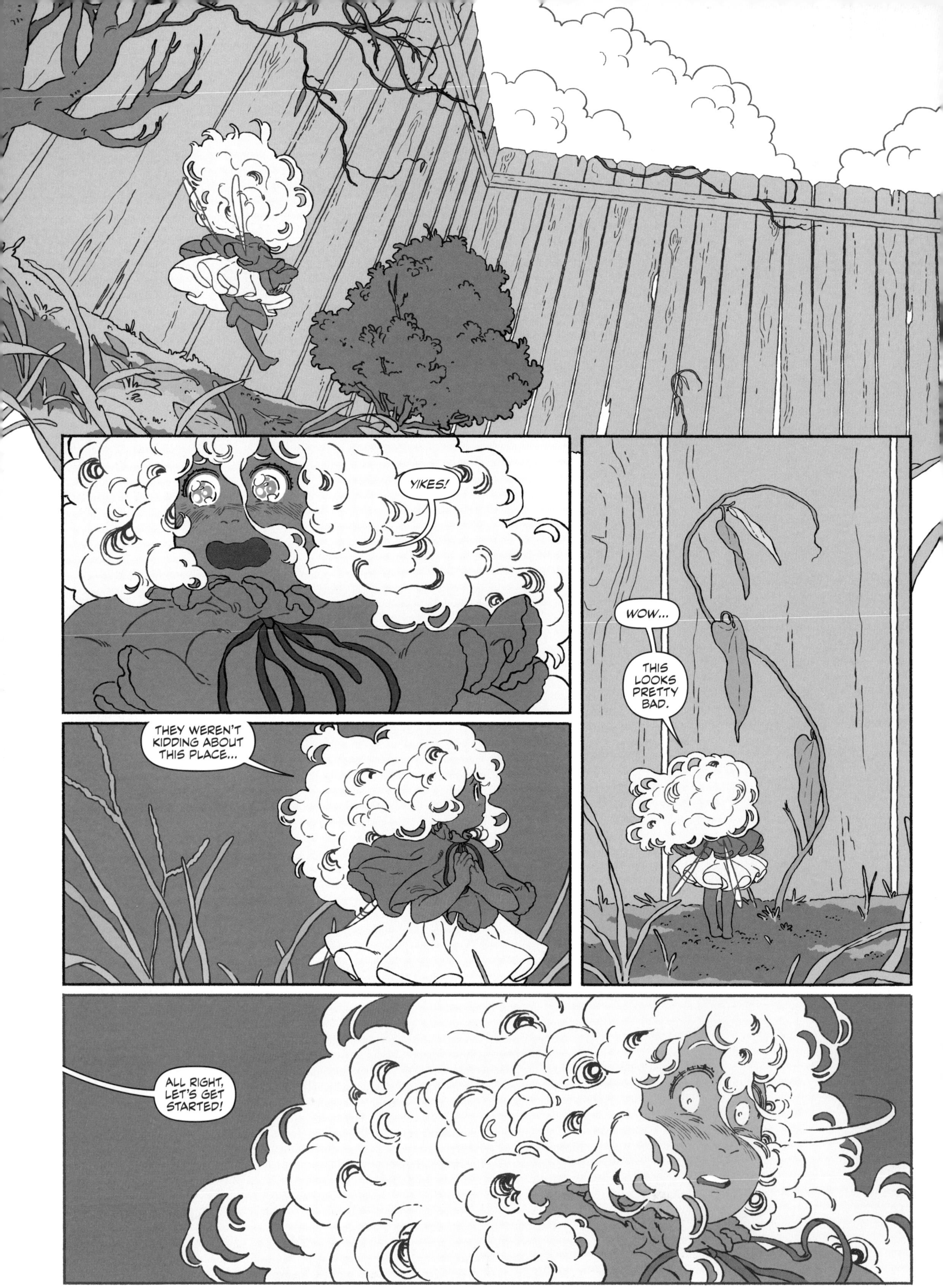
YIKES!
WOW...
THIS LOOKS PRETTY BAD.
THEY WEREN'T KIDDING ABOUT THIS PLACE...
ALL RIGHT, LET'S GET STARTED!

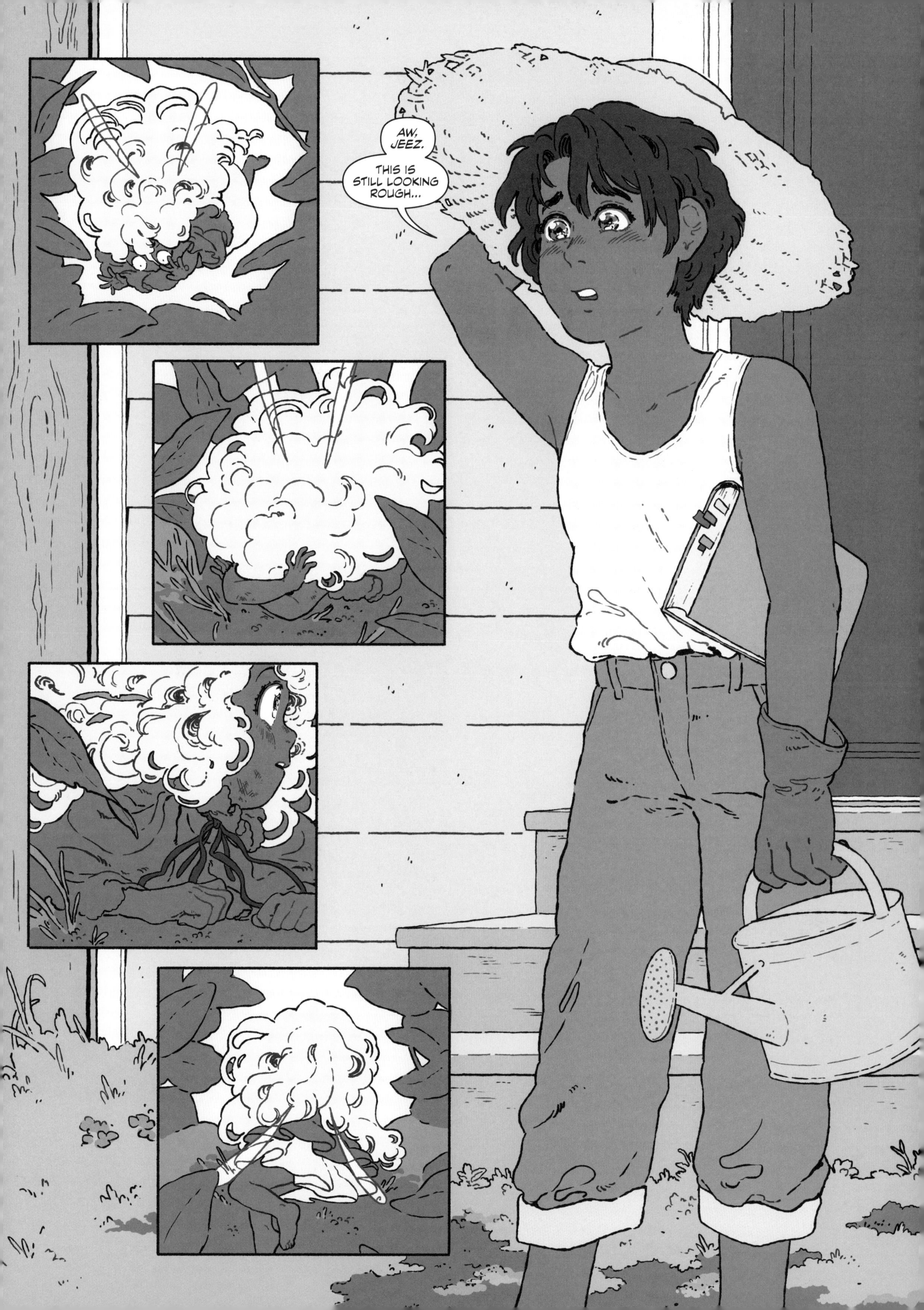
AW, JEEZ.
THIS IS STILL LOOKING ROUGH...

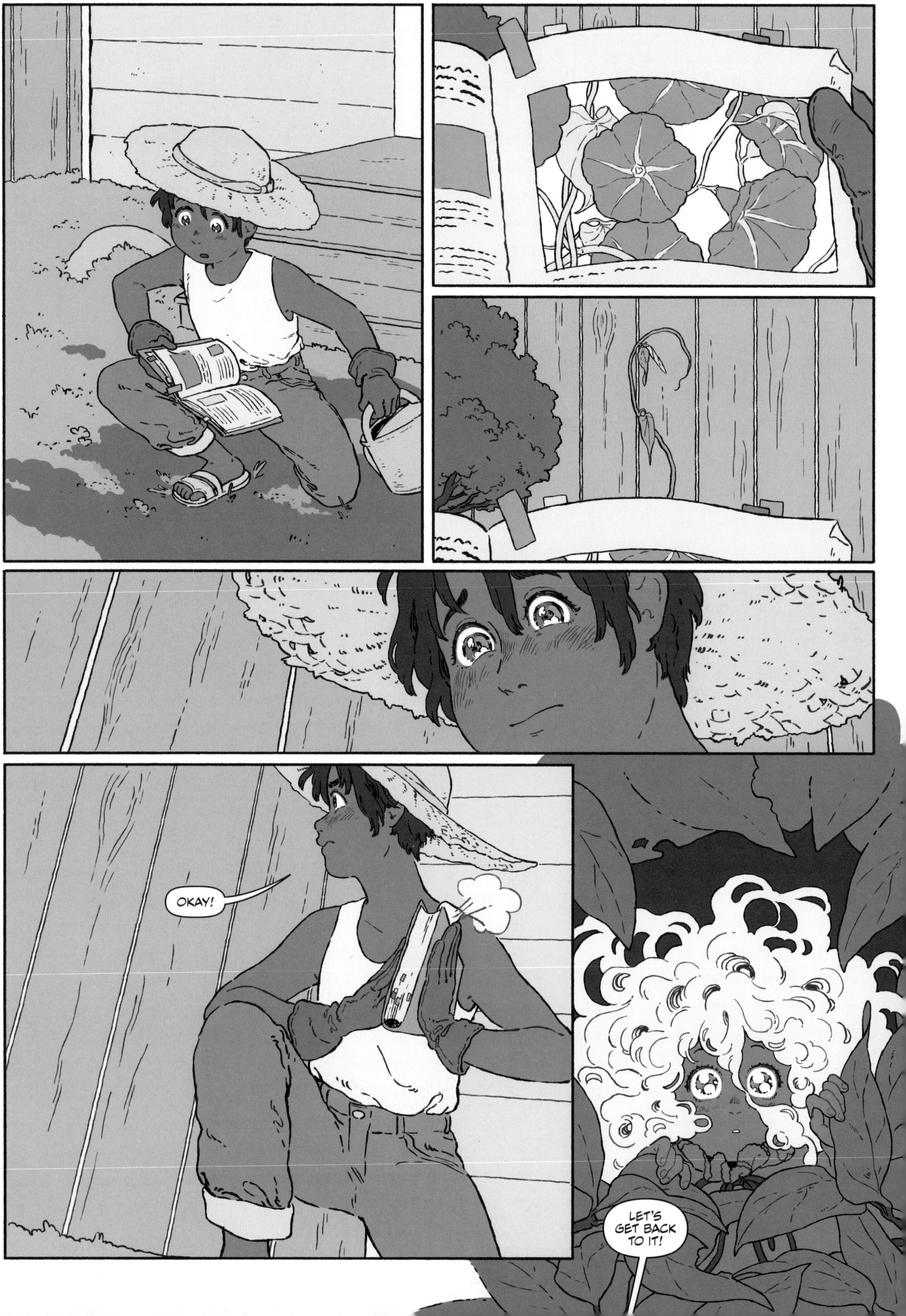
OKAY!
LET'S GET BACK TO IT!

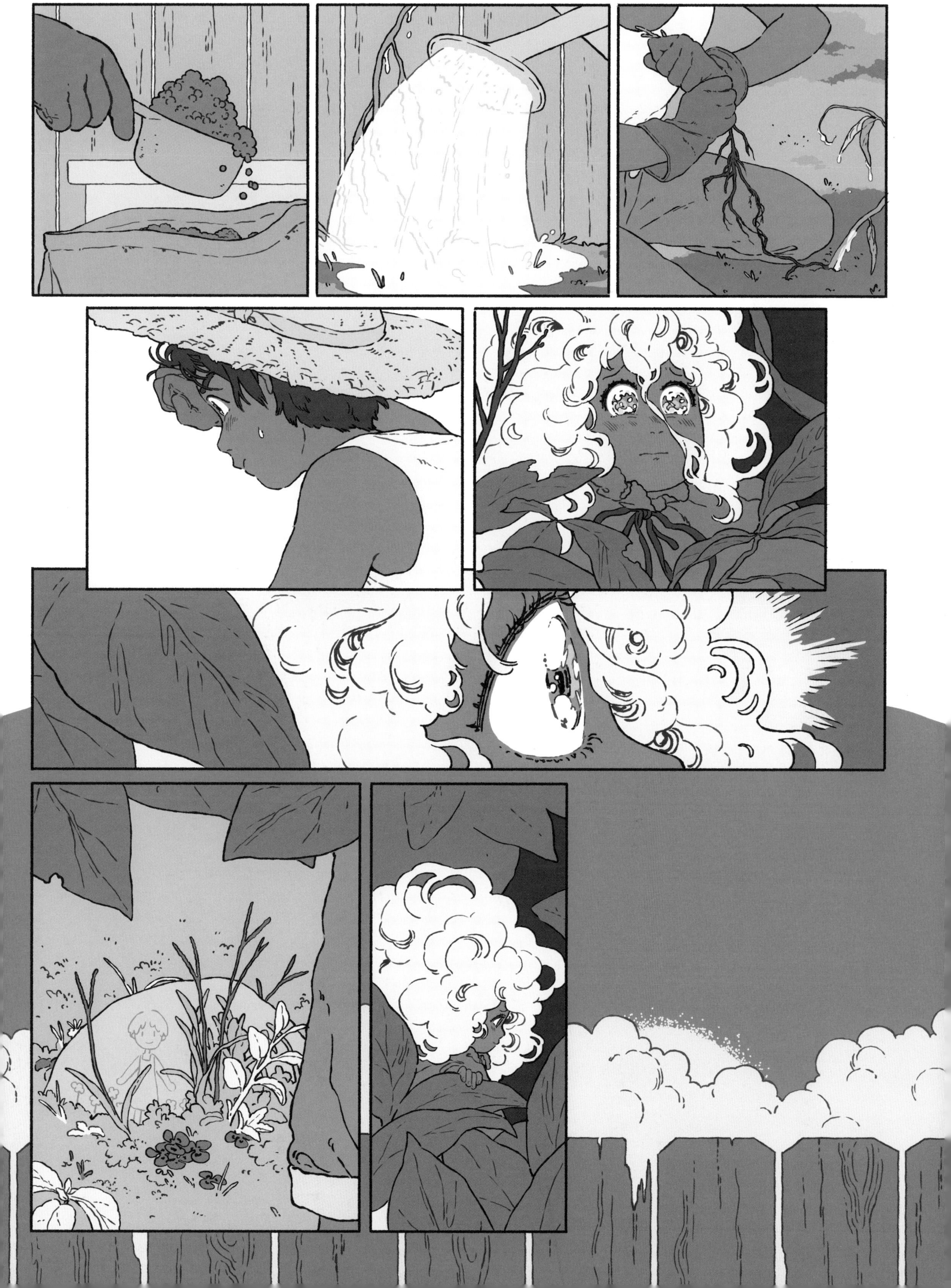

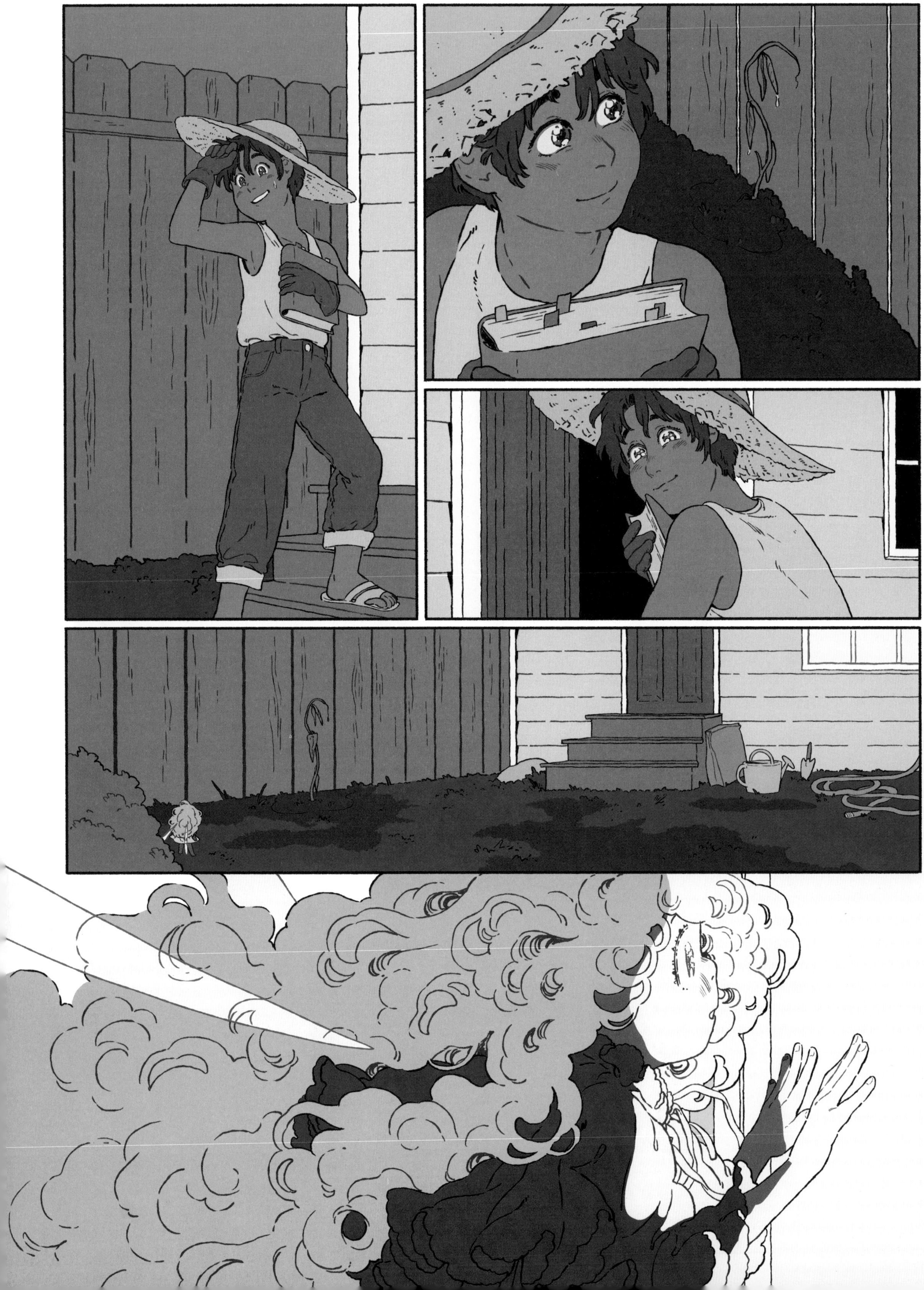

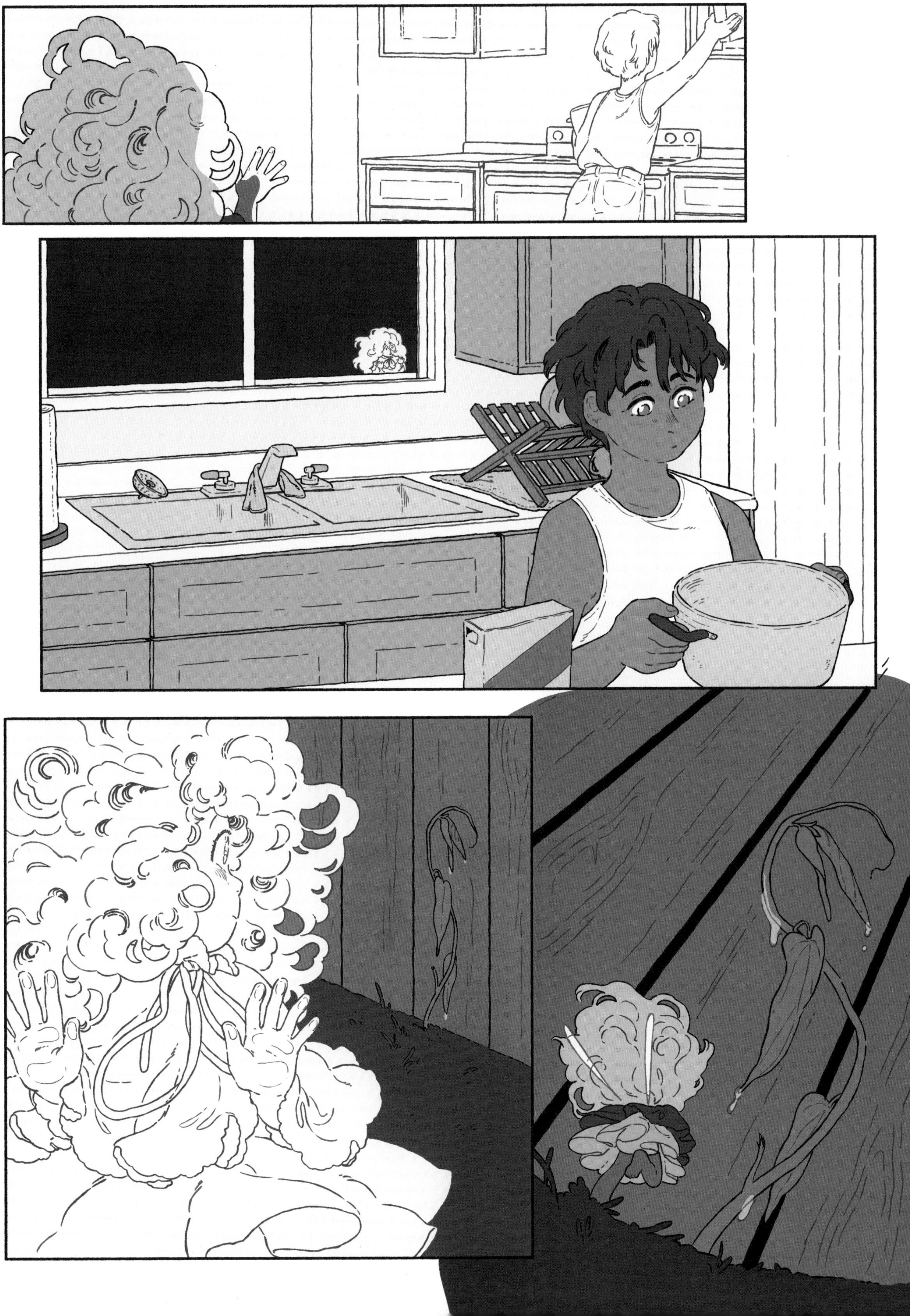

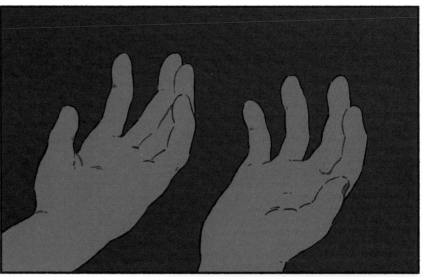

I GUESS I CAN'T, HUH...

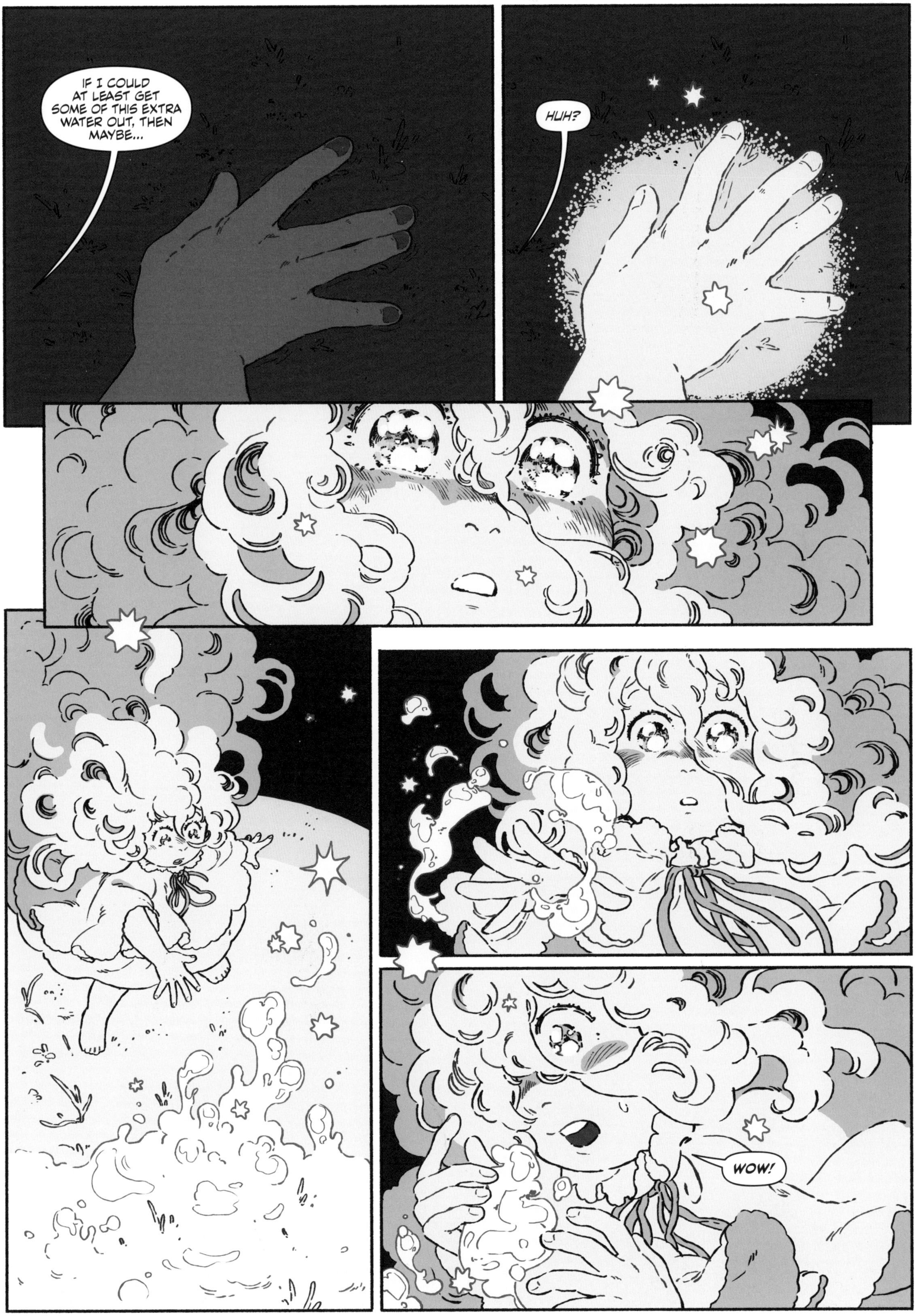
IF I COULD AT LEAST GET SOME OF THIS EXTRA WATER OUT, THEN MAYBE...
HUH?
WOW!

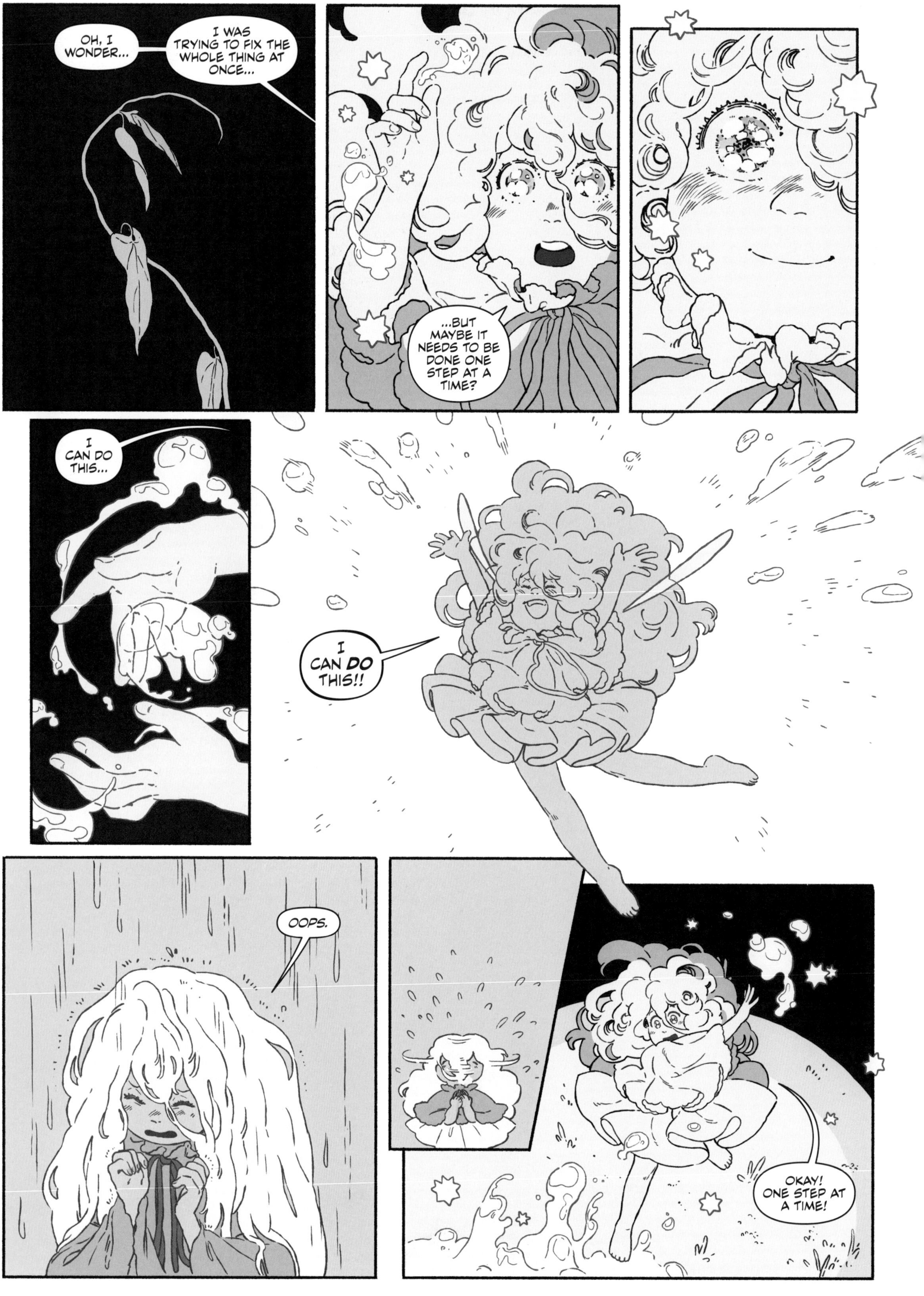
OH, I WONDER...
I WAS TRYING TO FIX THE WHOLE THING AT ONCE...
...BUT MAYBE IT NEEDS TO BE DONE ONE STEP AT A TIME?
I CAN DO THIS...
I CAN **DO** THIS!!
OOPS.
OKAY! ONE STEP AT A TIME!

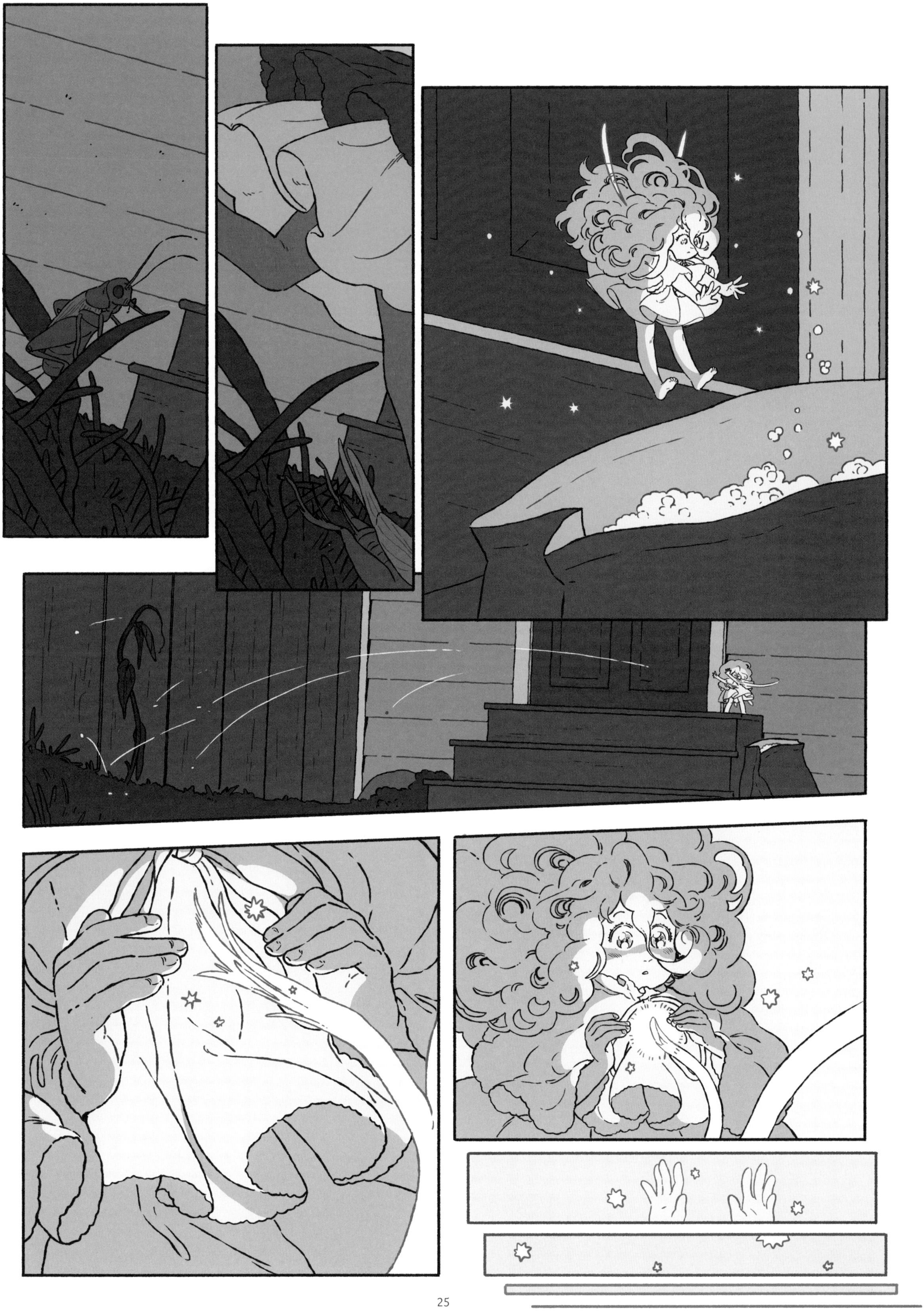

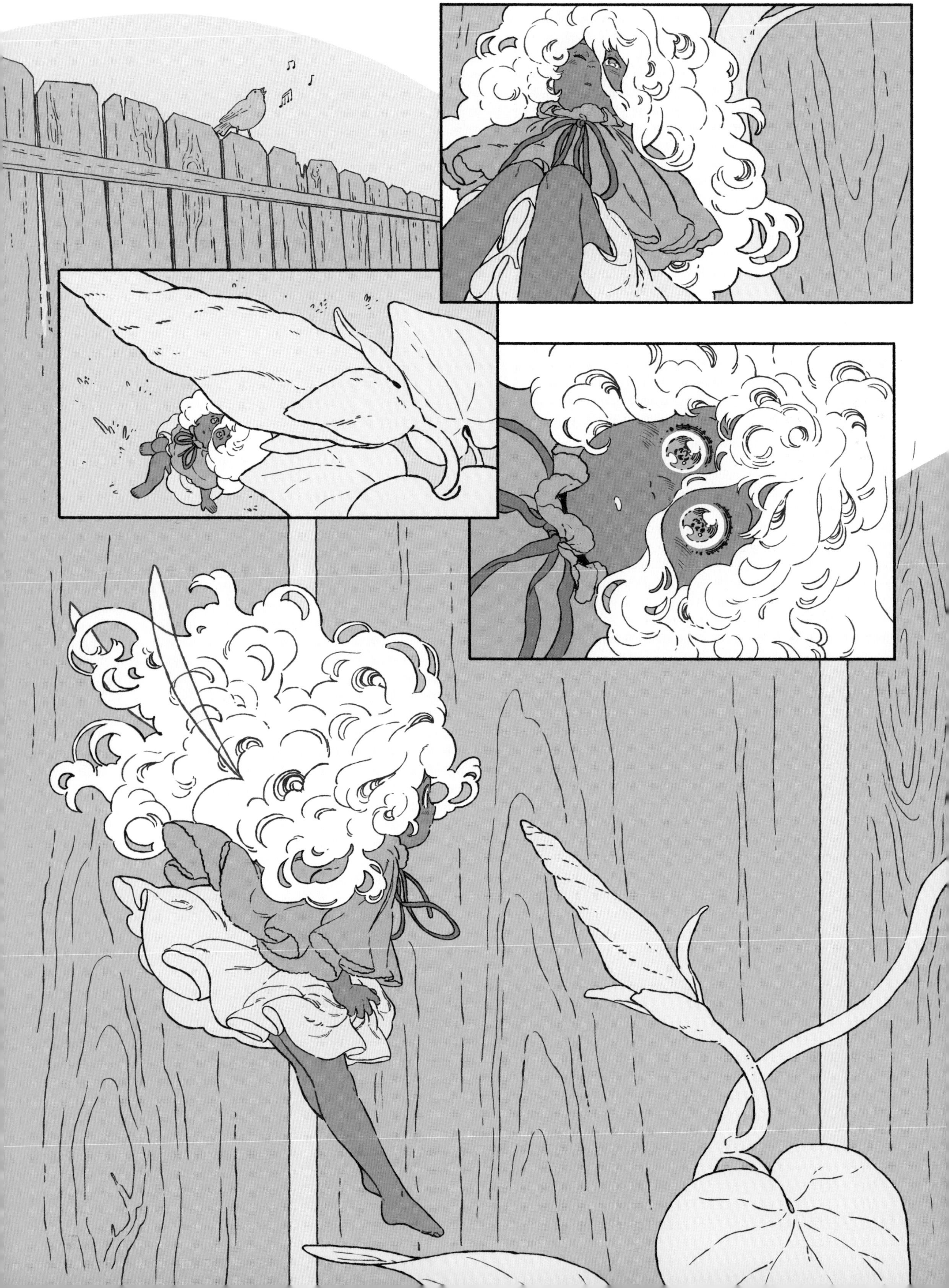

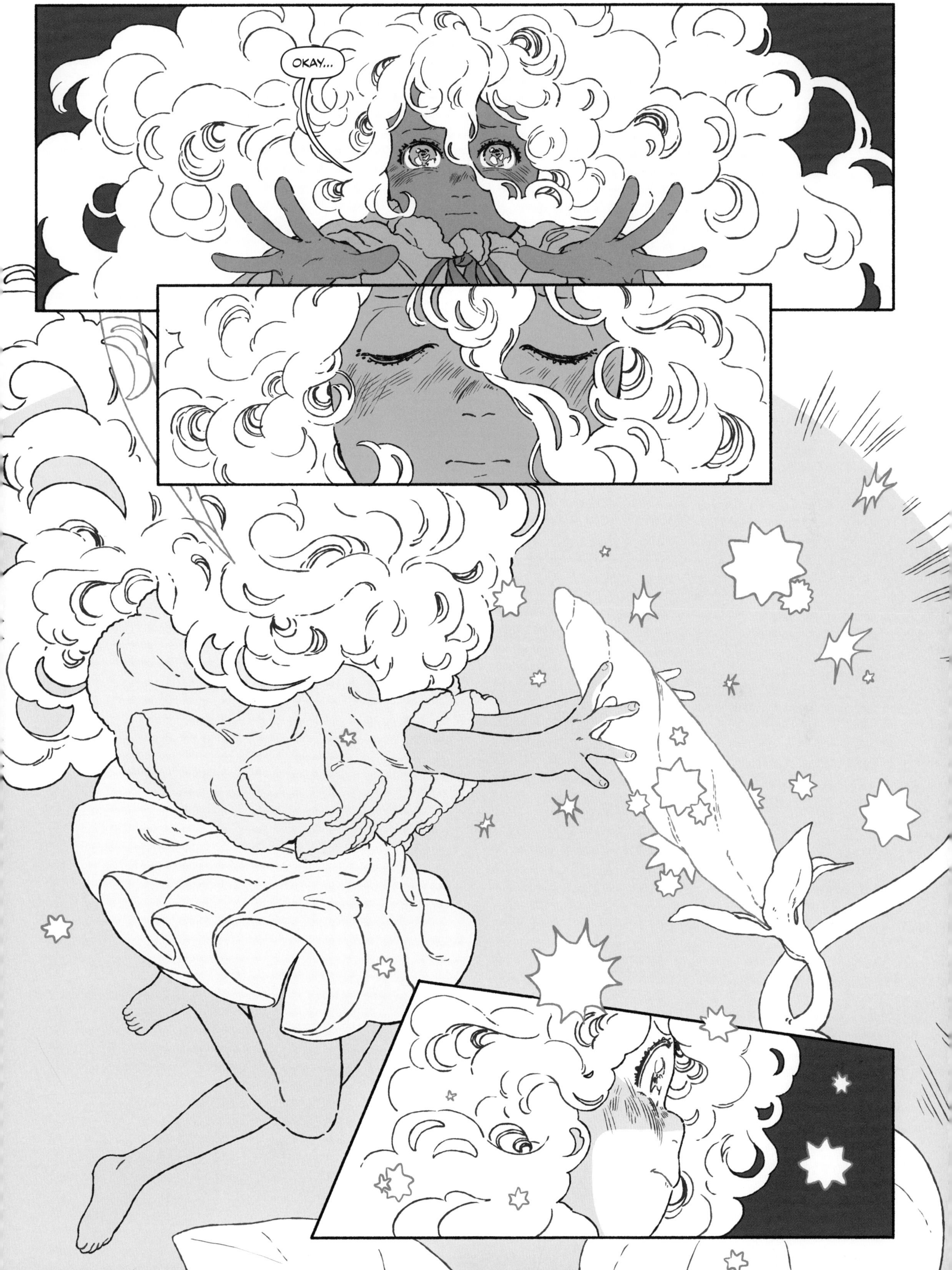
OKAY...

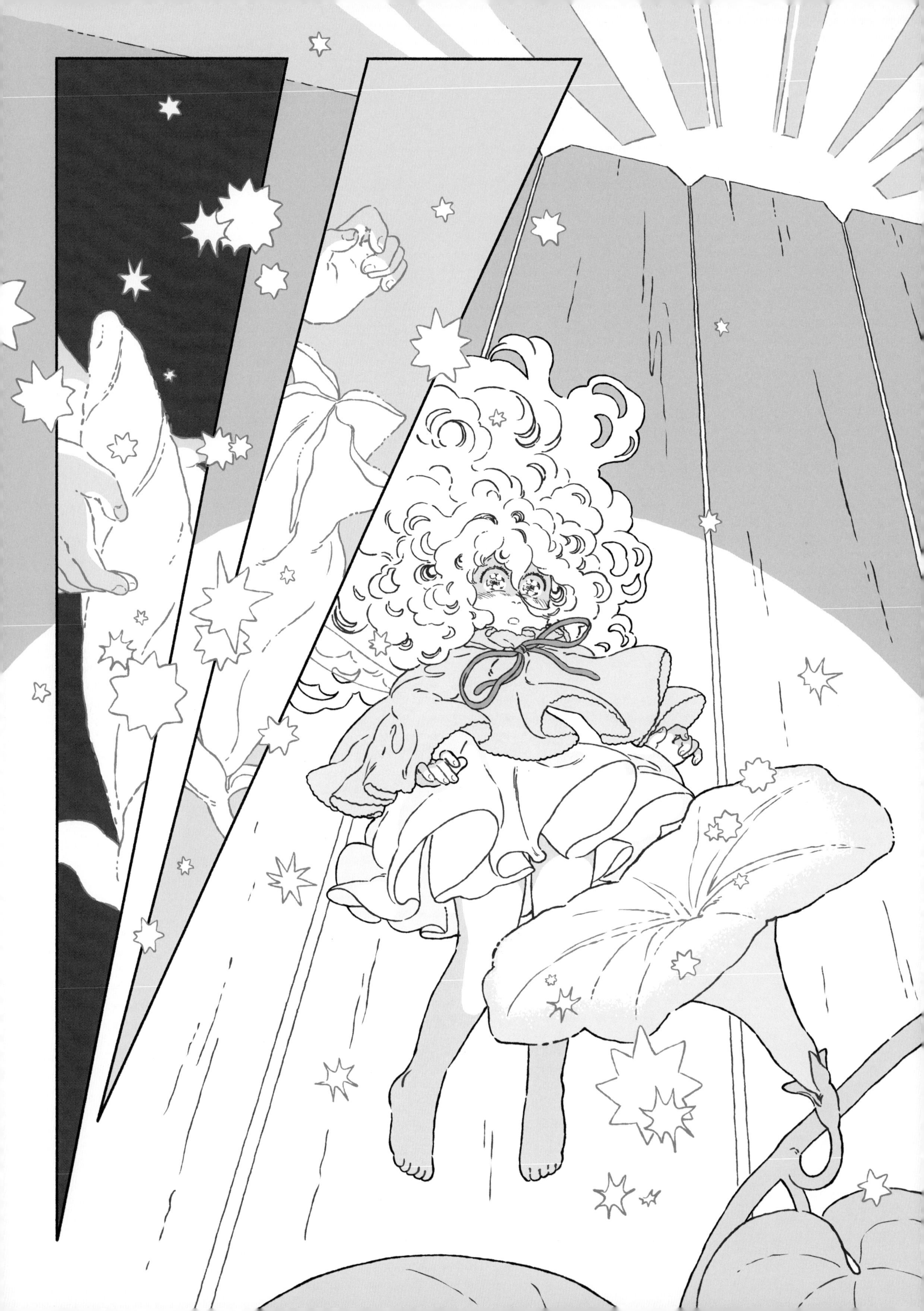

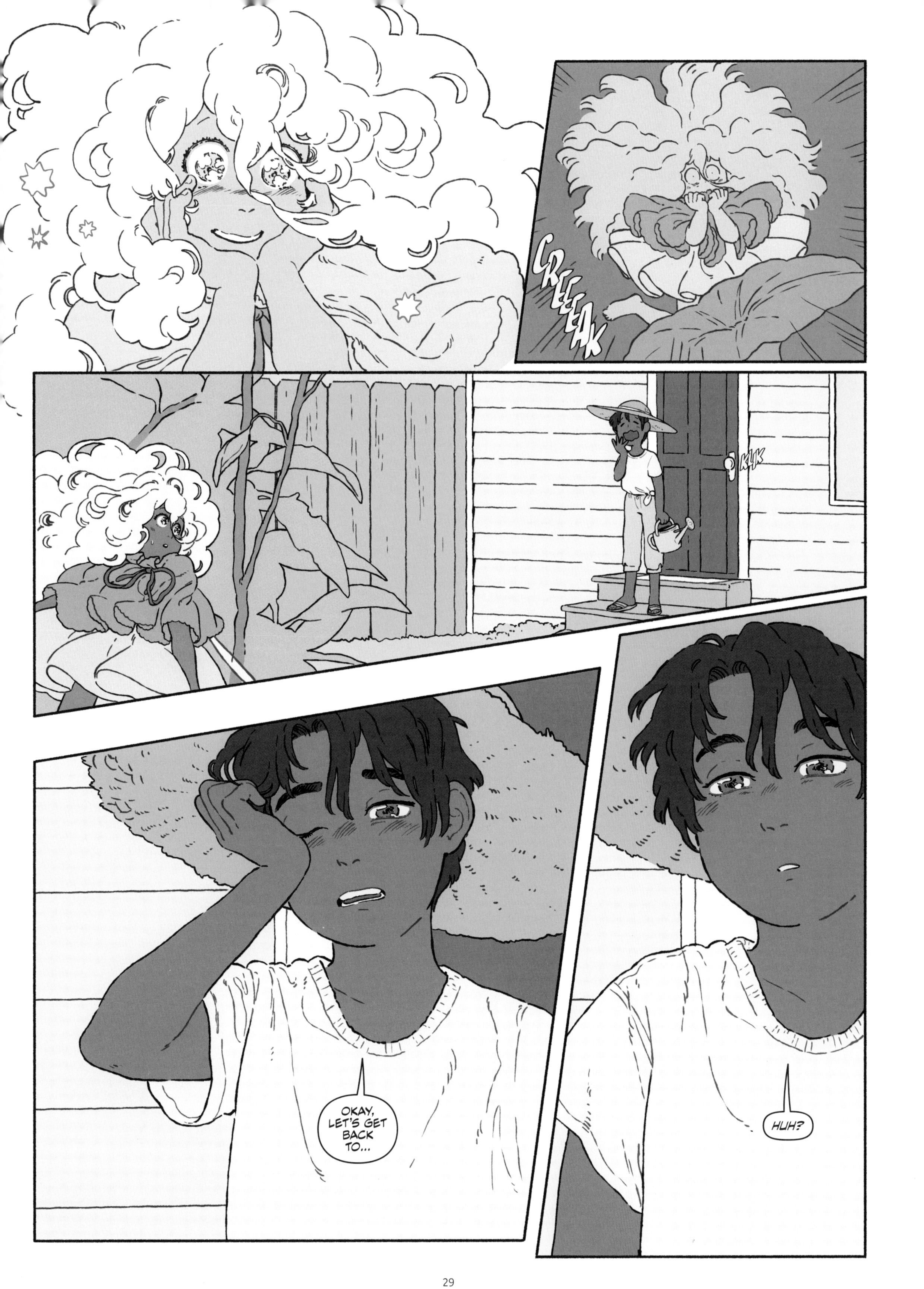
CREEEAK
KLIK
OKAY, LET'S GET BACK TO...
HUH?

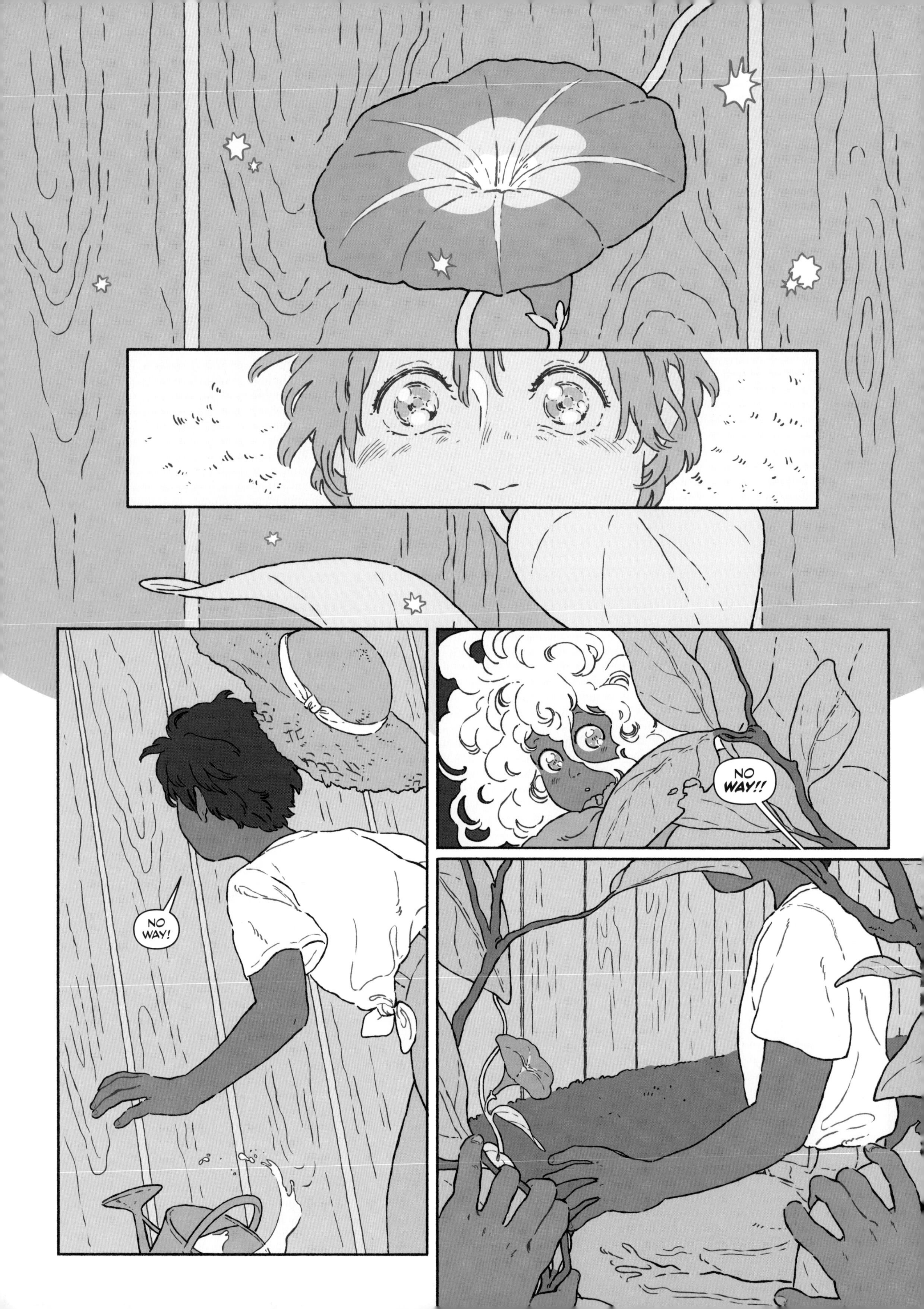
NO WAY!!
NO WAY!

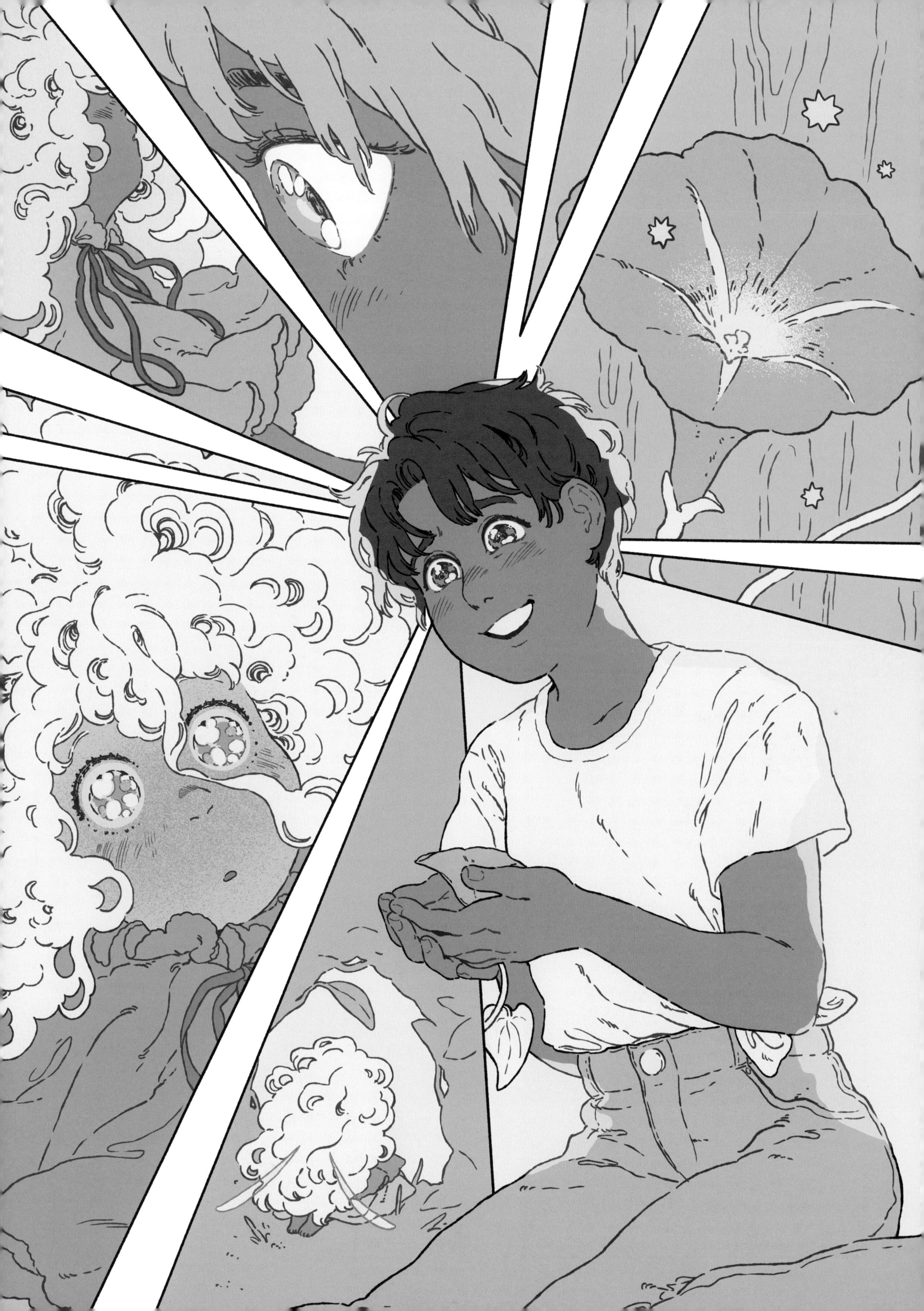

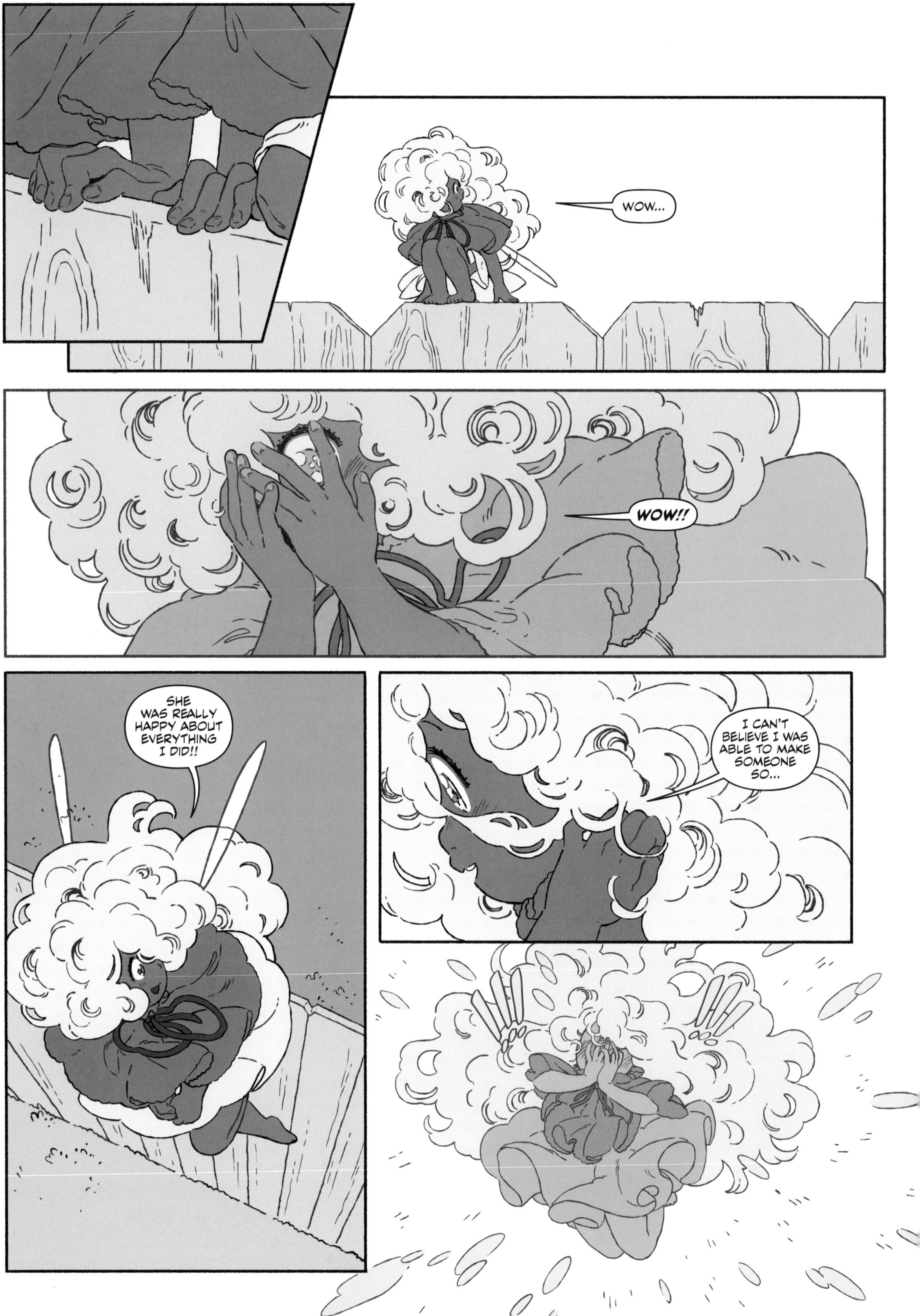
WOW...
WOW!!
SHE WAS REALLY HAPPY ABOUT EVERYTHING I DID!!
I CAN'T BELIEVE I WAS ABLE TO MAKE SOMEONE SO...

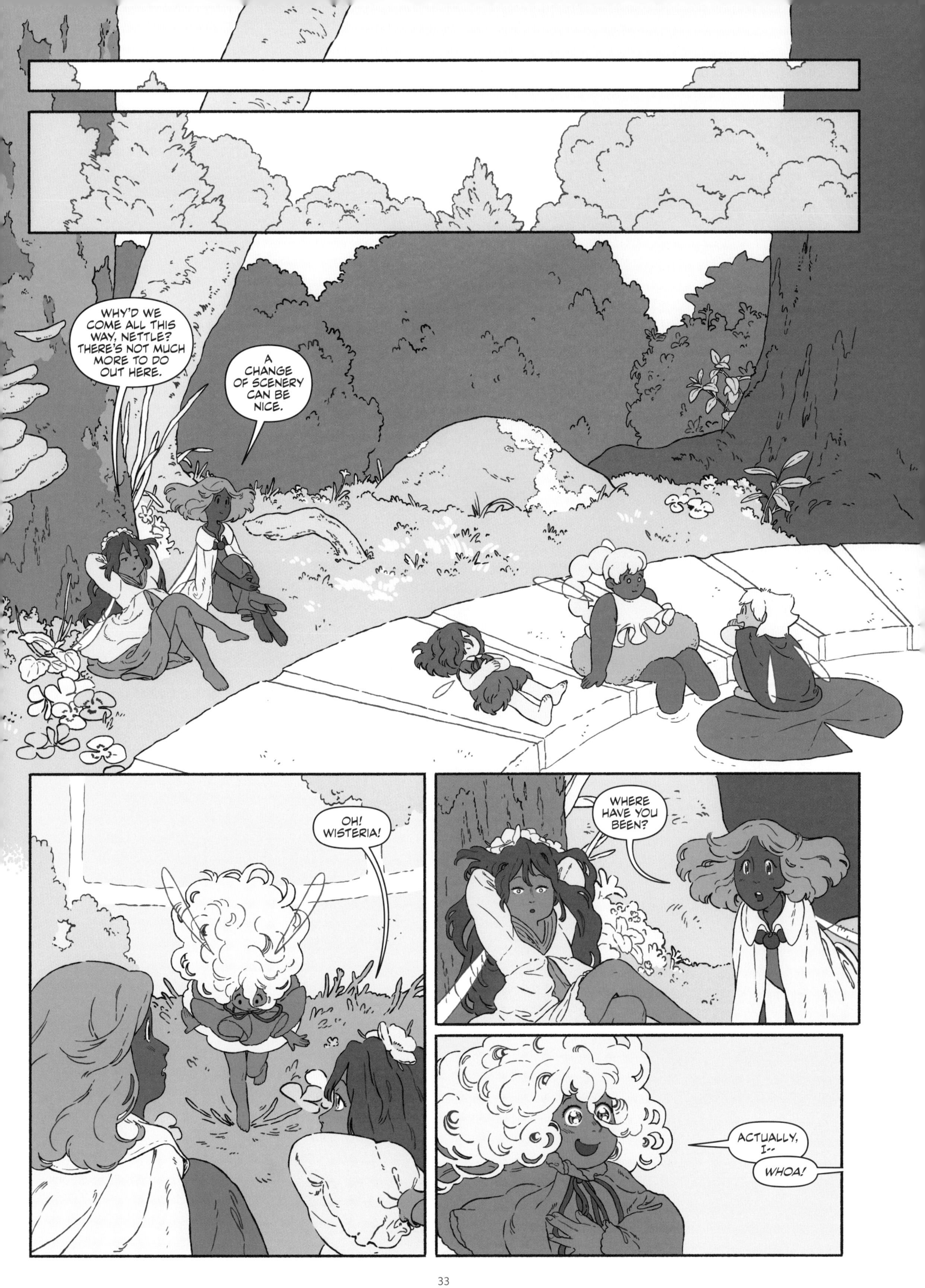
WHY'D WE COME ALL THIS WAY, NETTLE? THERE'S NOT MUCH MORE TO DO OUT HERE.
A CHANGE OF SCENERY CAN BE NICE.
OH! WISTERIA!
WHERE HAVE YOU BEEN?
ACTUALLY, I--
WHOA!

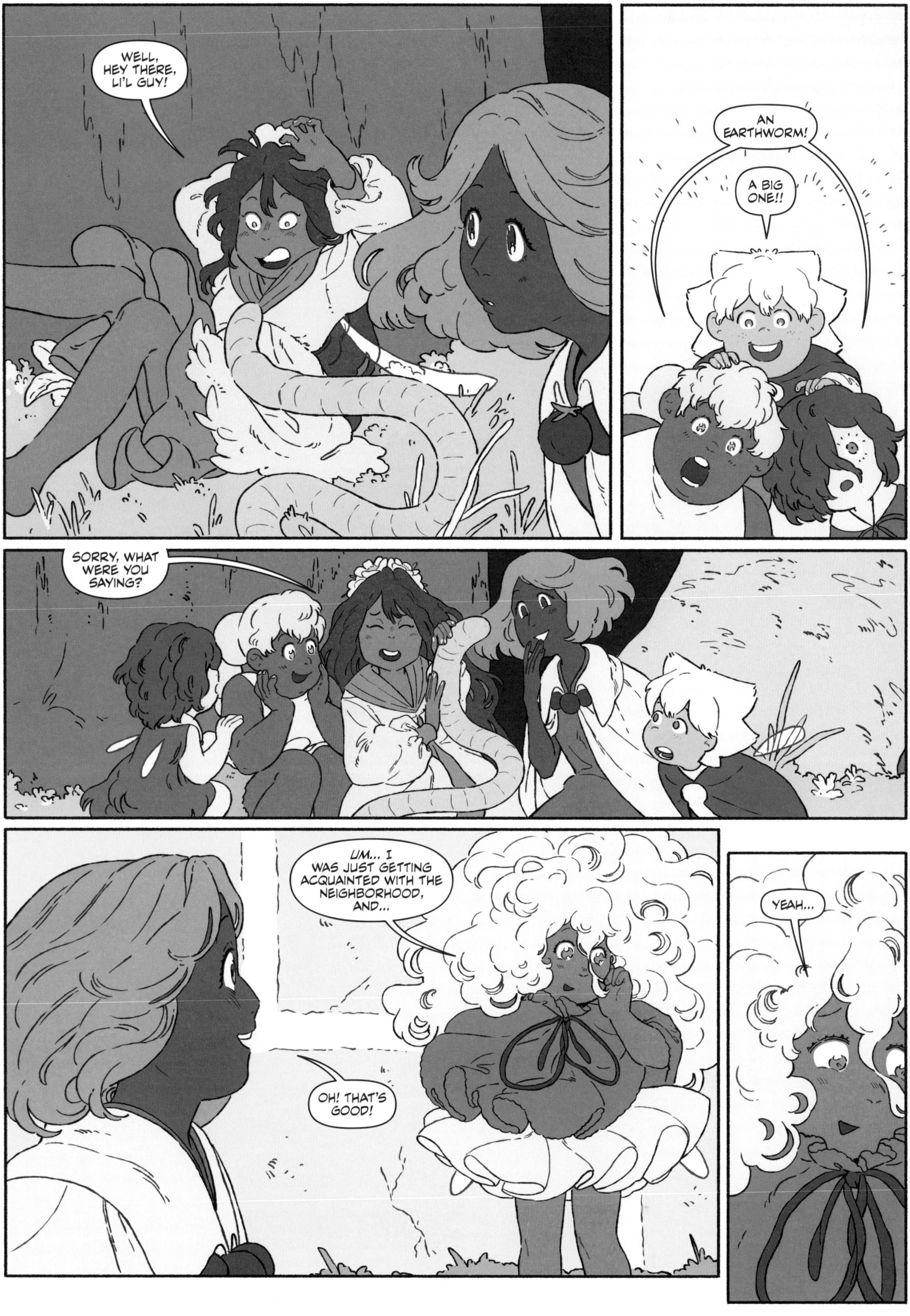

WELL, HEY THERE, LI'L GUY!
AN EARTHWORM!
A BIG ONE!!
SORRY, WHAT WERE YOU SAYING?
UM... I WAS JUST GETTING ACQUAINTED WITH THE NEIGHBORHOOD, AND...
OH! THAT'S GOOD!
YEAH...

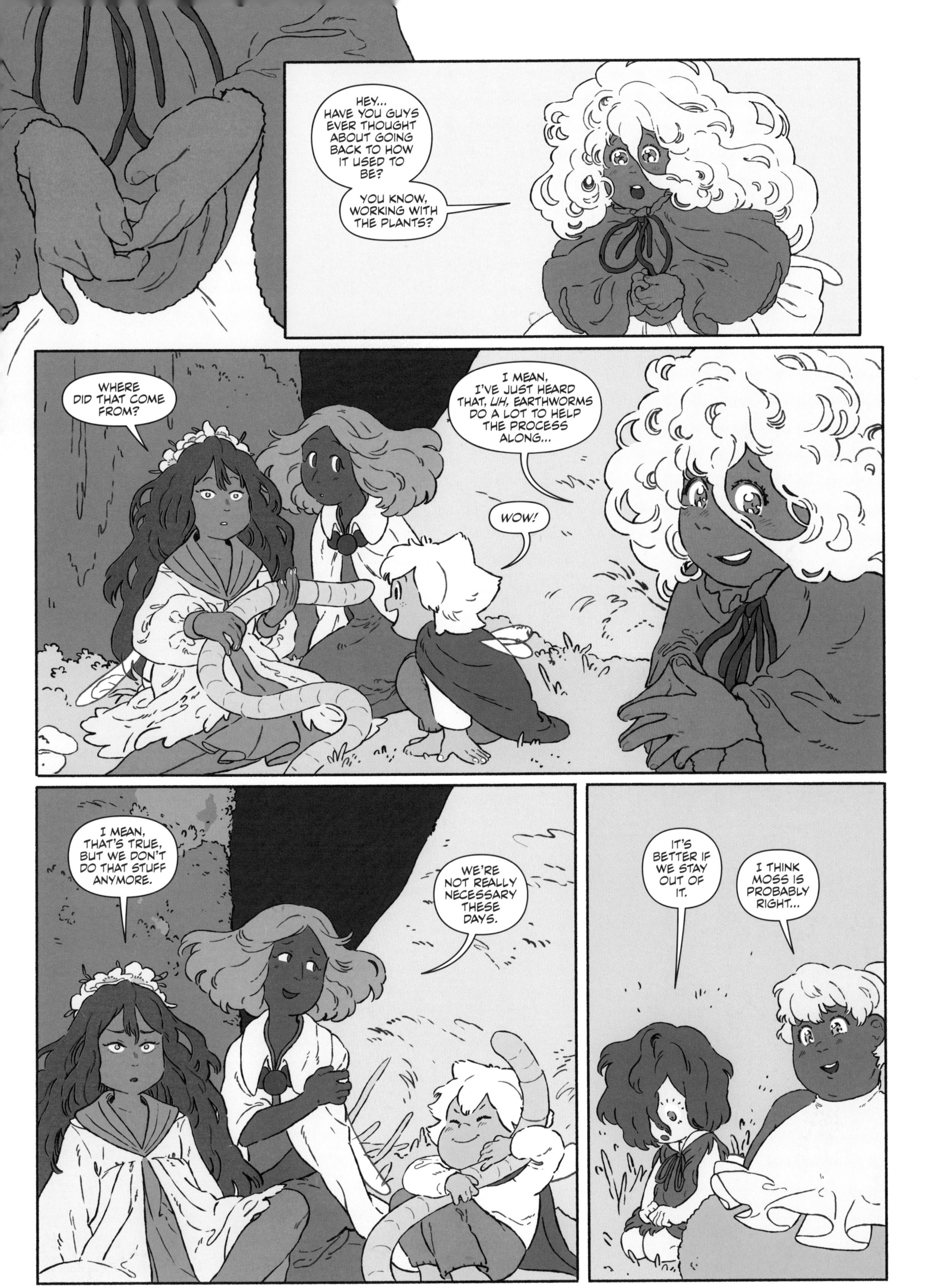
HEY... HAVE YOU GUYS EVER THOUGHT ABOUT GOING BACK TO HOW IT USED TO BE?
YOU KNOW, WORKING WITH THE PLANTS?
WHERE DID THAT COME FROM?
I MEAN, I'VE JUST HEARD THAT, *UH*, EARTHWORMS DO A LOT TO HELP THE PROCESS ALONG...
WOW!
I MEAN, THAT'S TRUE, BUT WE DON'T DO THAT STUFF ANYMORE.
WE'RE NOT REALLY NECESSARY THESE DAYS.
I THINK MOSS IS PROBABLY RIGHT...
IT'S BETTER IF WE STAY OUT OF IT.

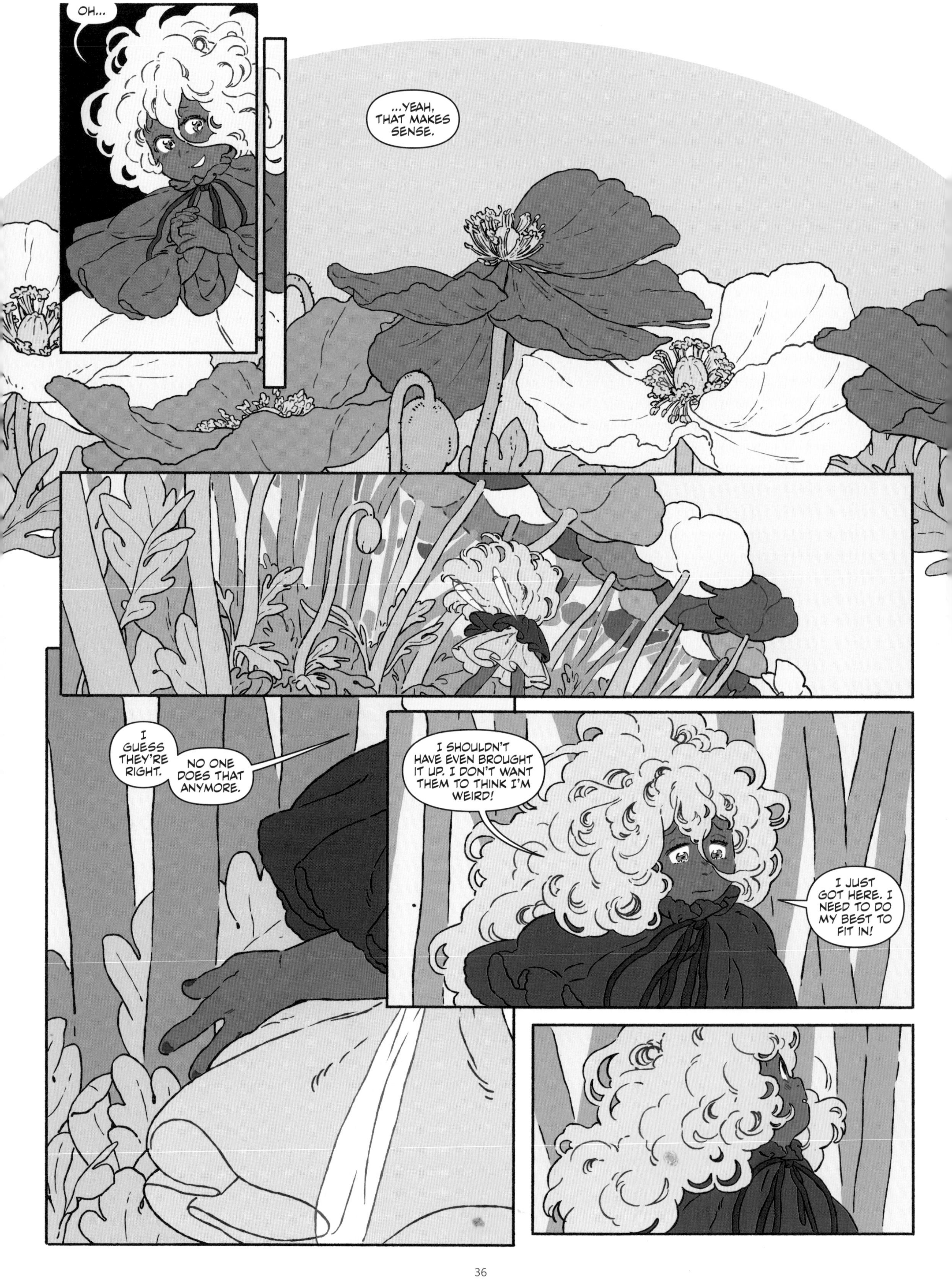
OH...
...YEAH, THAT MAKES SENSE.
I GUESS THEY'RE RIGHT.
NO ONE DOES THAT ANYMORE.
I SHOULDN'T HAVE EVEN BROUGHT IT UP. I DON'T WANT THEM TO THINK I'M WEIRD!
I JUST GOT HERE. I NEED TO DO MY BEST TO FIT IN!

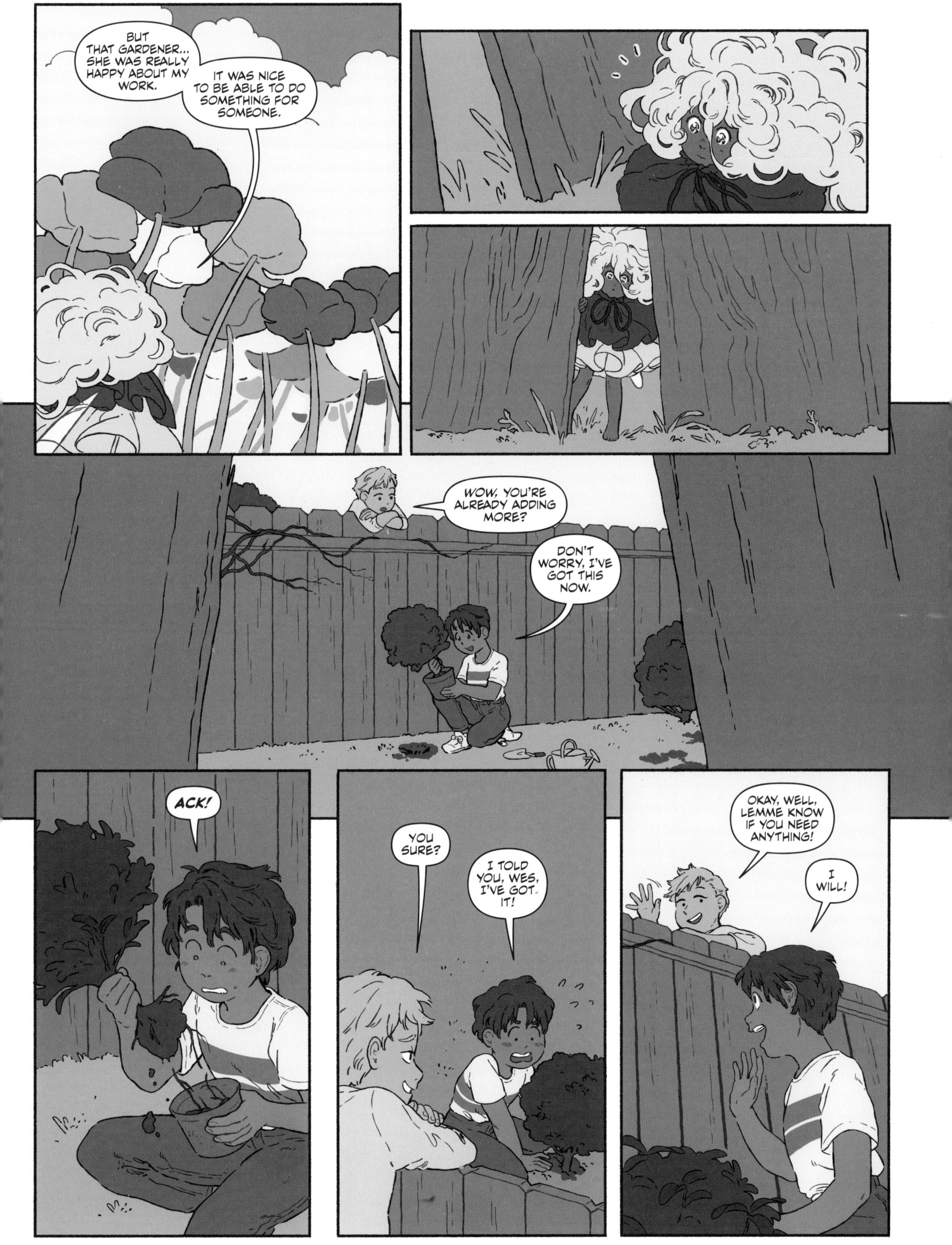

BUT THAT GARDENER... SHE WAS REALLY HAPPY ABOUT MY WORK.
IT WAS NICE TO BE ABLE TO DO SOMETHING FOR SOMEONE.
WOW, YOU'RE ALREADY ADDING MORE?
DON'T WORRY, I'VE GOT THIS NOW.
ACK!
YOU SURE?
I TOLD YOU, WES, I'VE GOT IT!
OKAY, WELL, LEMME KNOW IF YOU NEED ANYTHING!
I WILL!

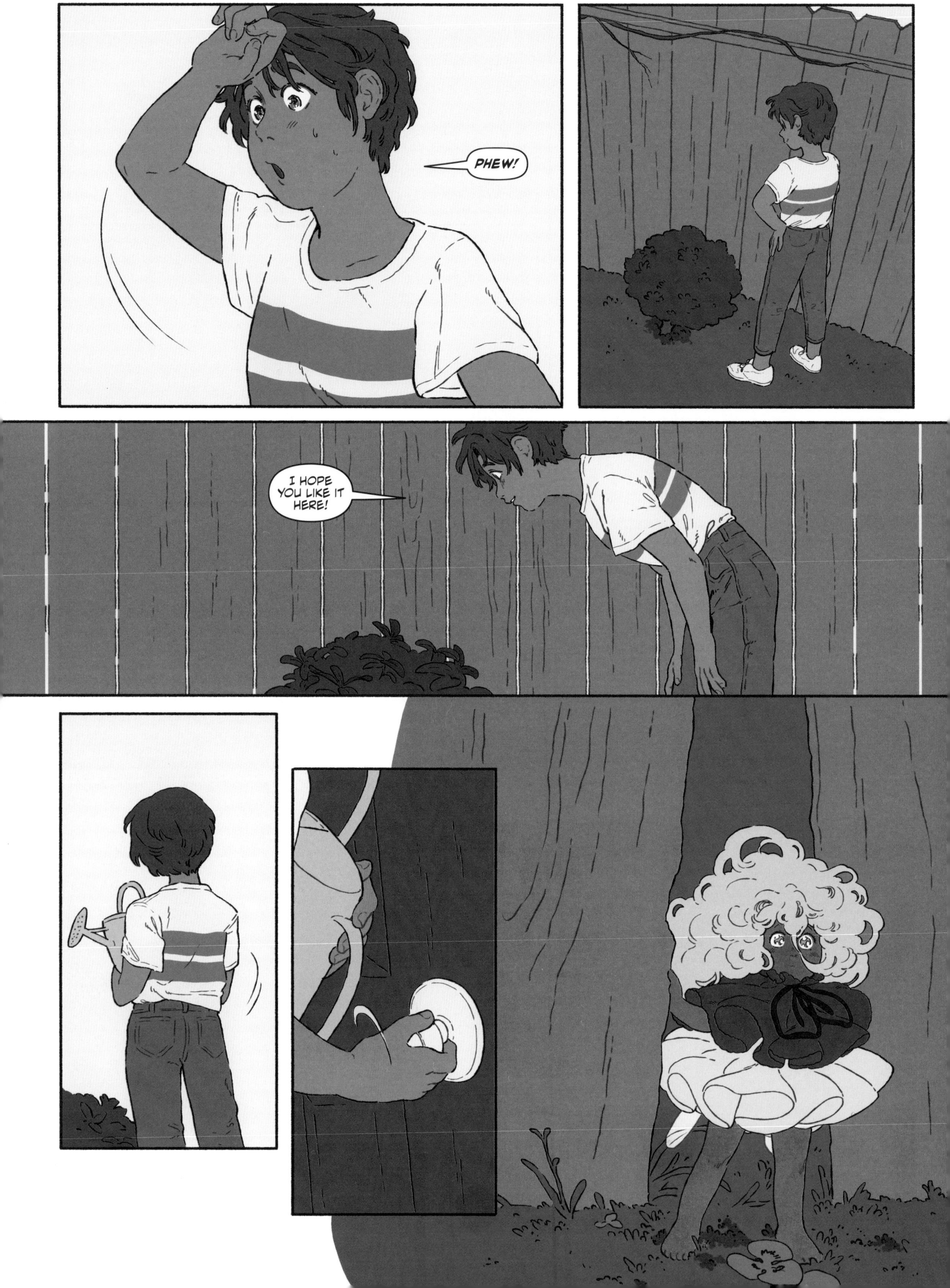
PHEW!
I HOPE YOU LIKE IT HERE!

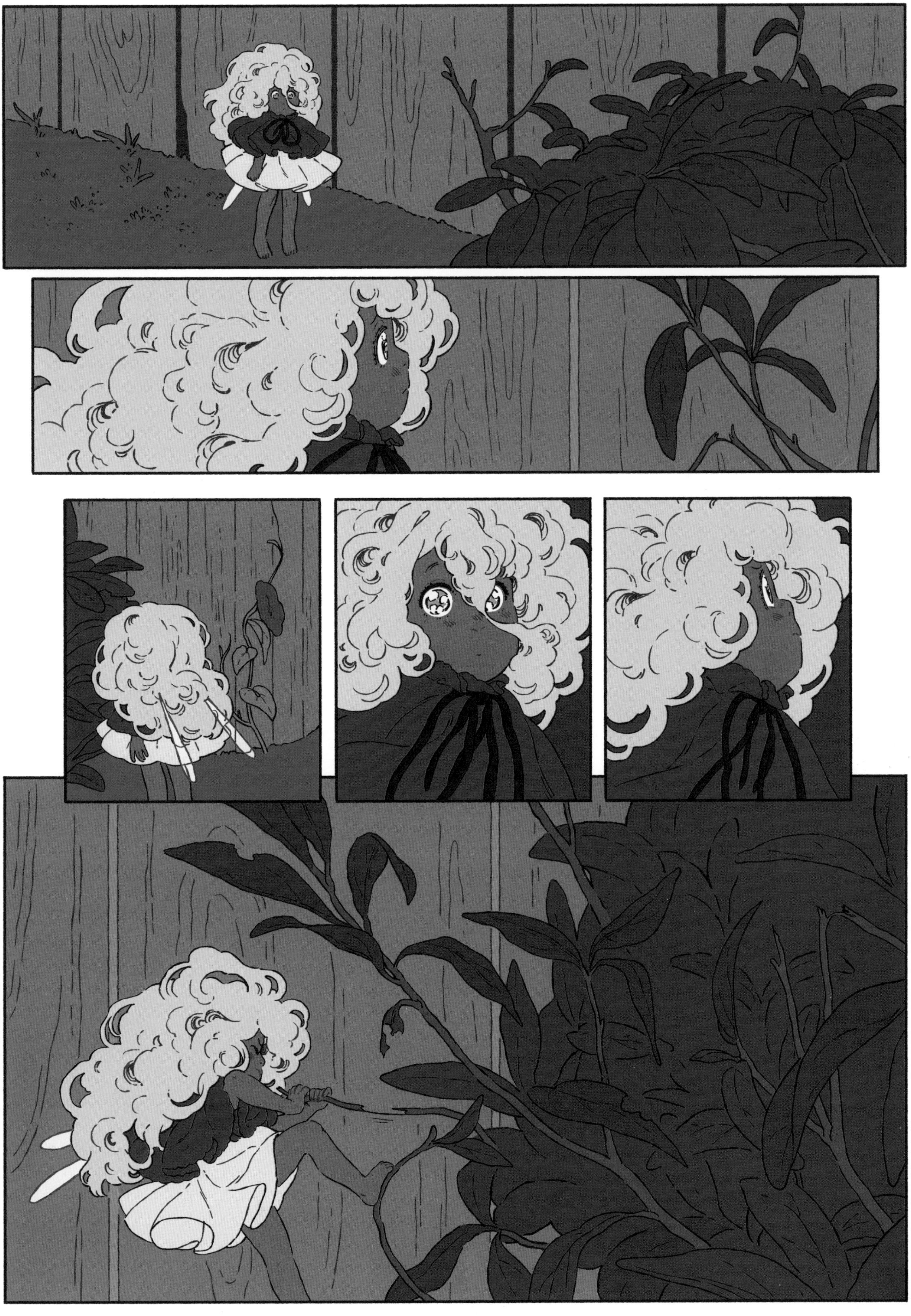

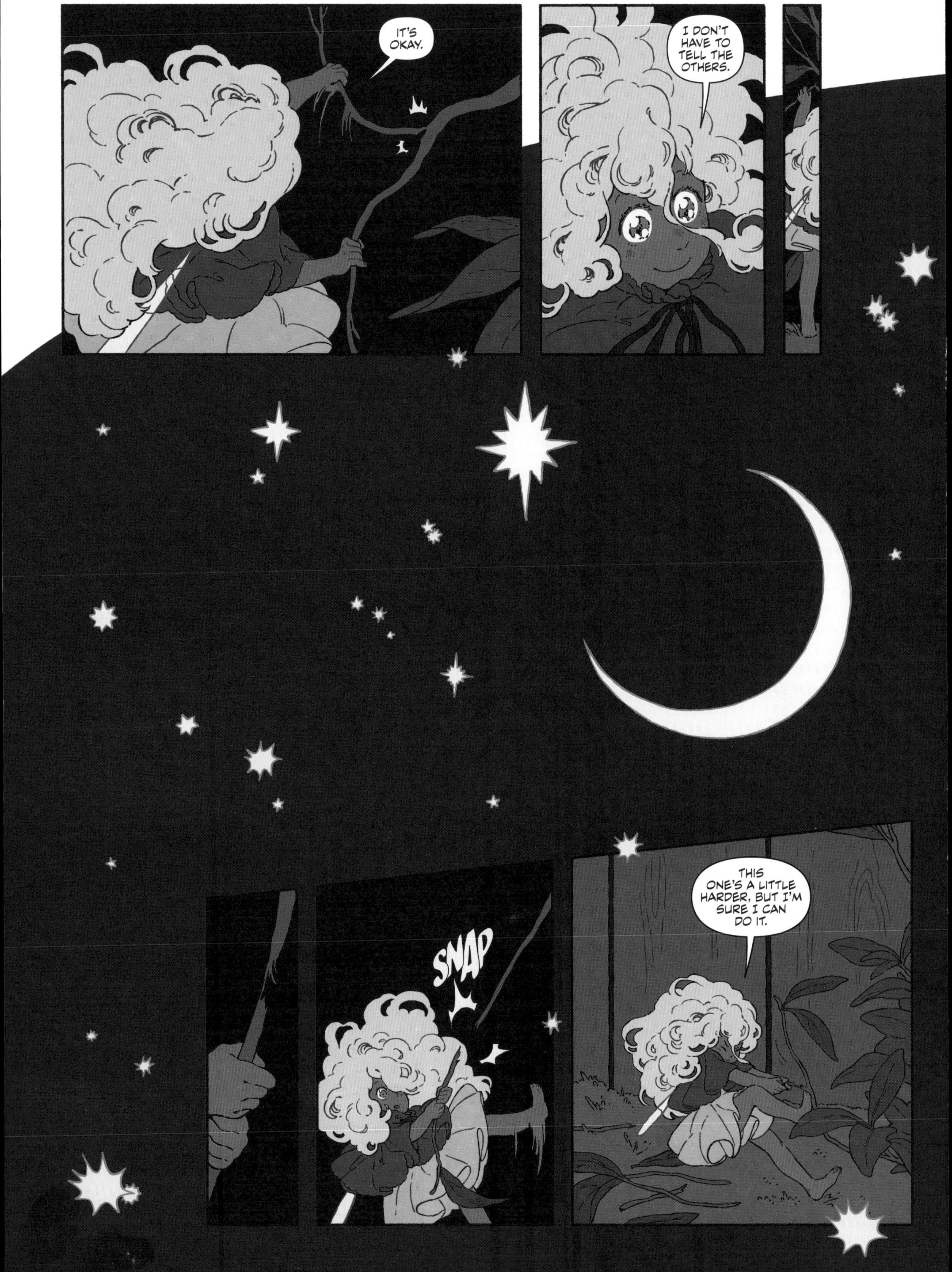
IT'S OKAY.
I DON'T HAVE TO TELL THE OTHERS.
SNAP
THIS ONE'S A LITTLE HARDER, BUT I'M SURE I CAN DO IT.

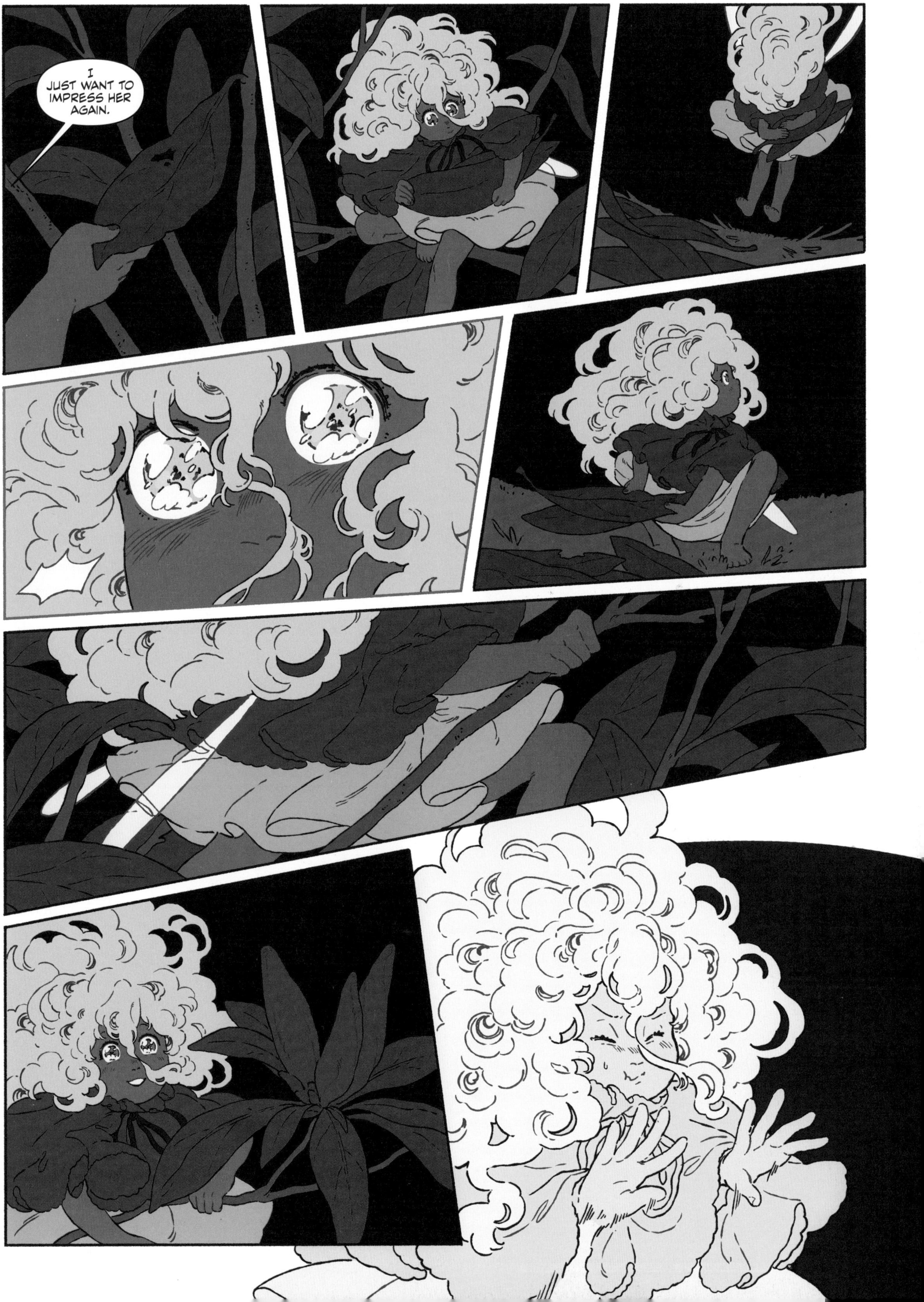
I JUST WANT TO IMPRESS HER AGAIN.

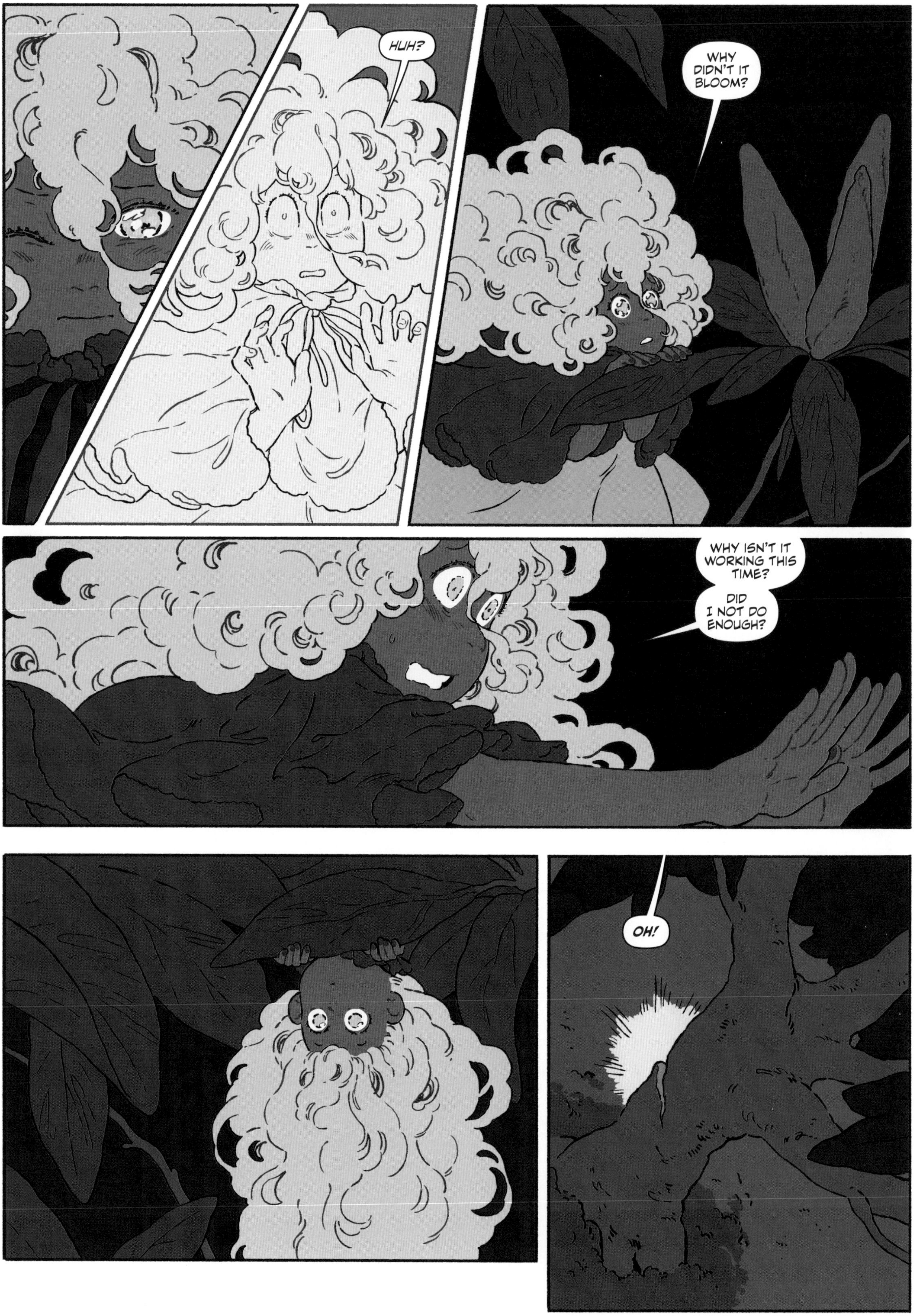
HUH?
WHY DIDN'T IT BLOOM?
WHY ISN'T IT WORKING THIS TIME?
DID I NOT DO ENOUGH?
OH!

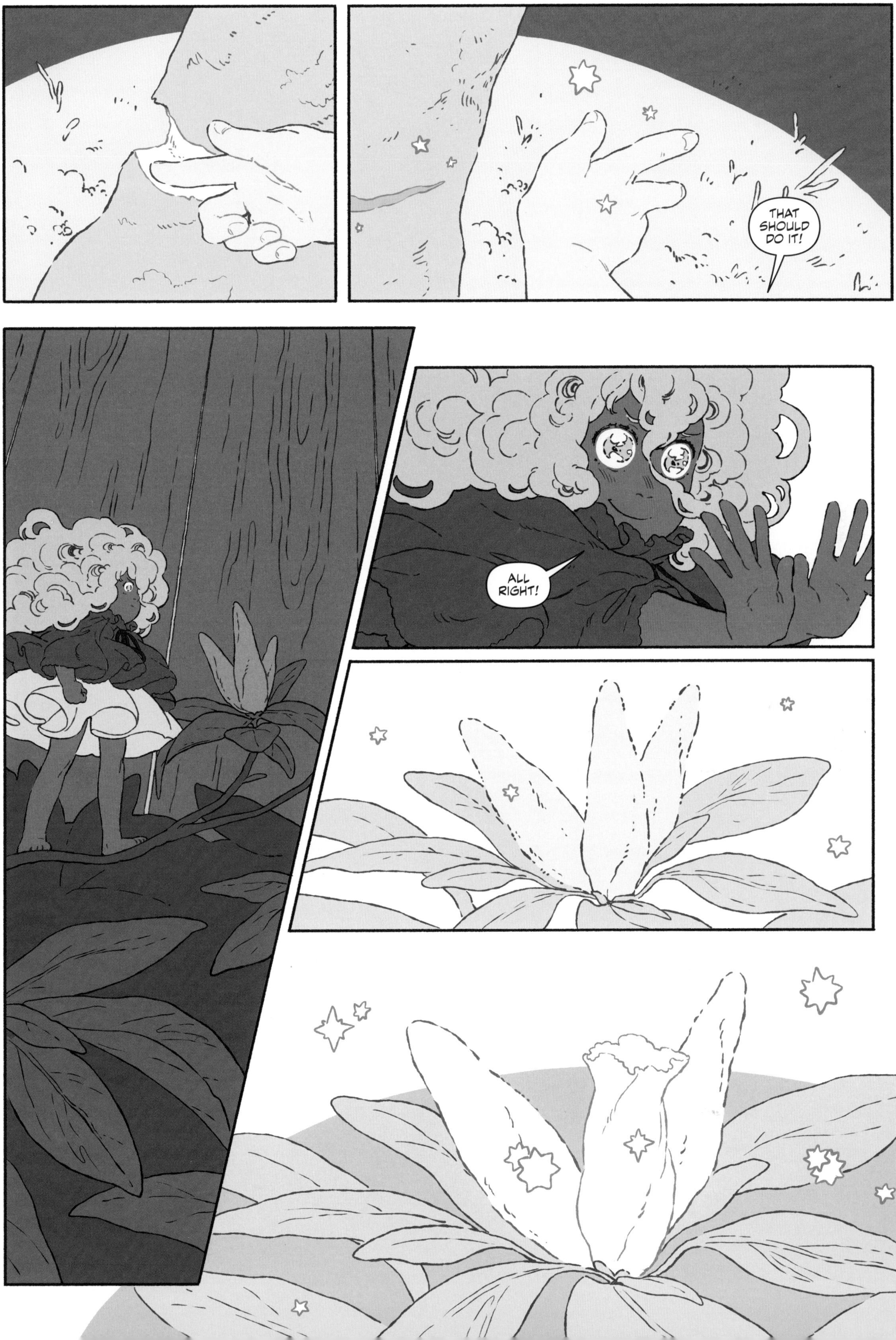
THAT SHOULD DO IT!
ALL RIGHT!

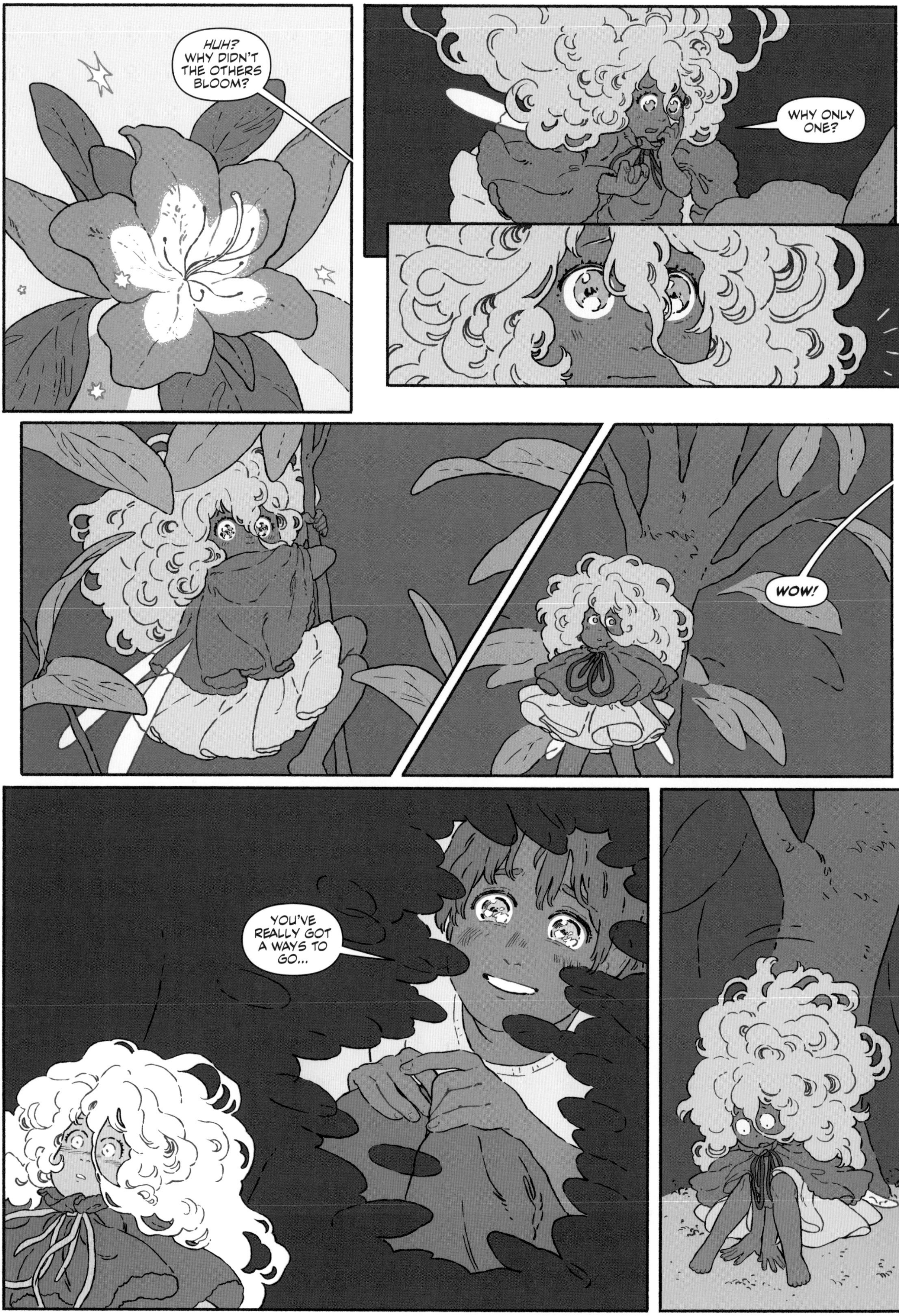
HUH? WHY DIDN'T THE OTHERS BLOOM?
WHY ONLY ONE?
WOW!
YOU'VE REALLY GOT A WAYS TO GO...

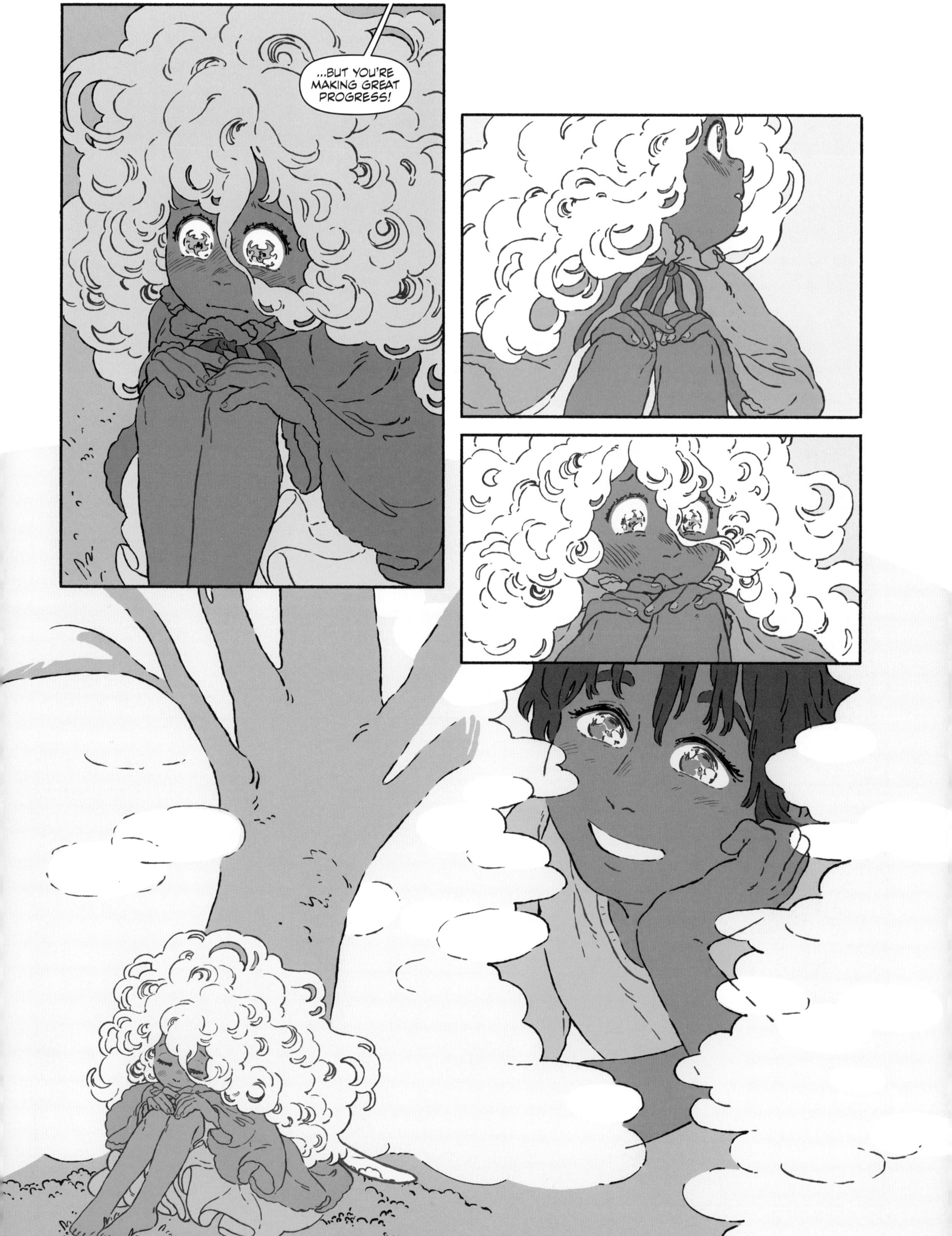
...BUT YOU'RE MAKING GREAT PROGRESS!

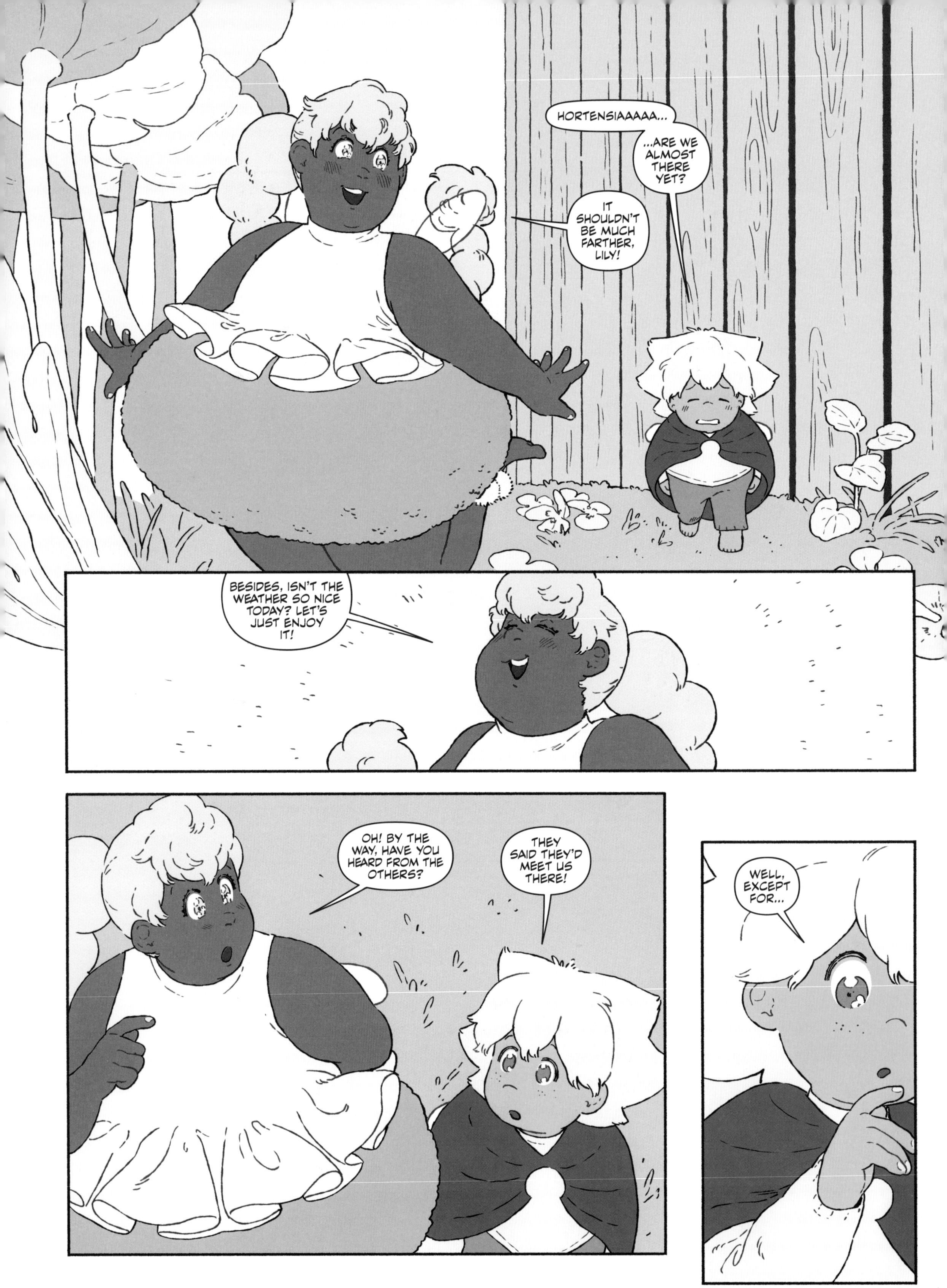
HORTENSIAAAAA...
...ARE WE ALMOST THERE YET?
IT SHOULDN'T BE MUCH FARTHER, LILY!
BESIDES, ISN'T THE WEATHER SO NICE TODAY? LET'S JUST ENJOY IT!
OH! BY THE WAY, HAVE YOU HEARD FROM THE OTHERS?
THEY SAID THEY'D MEET US THERE!
WELL, EXCEPT FOR...

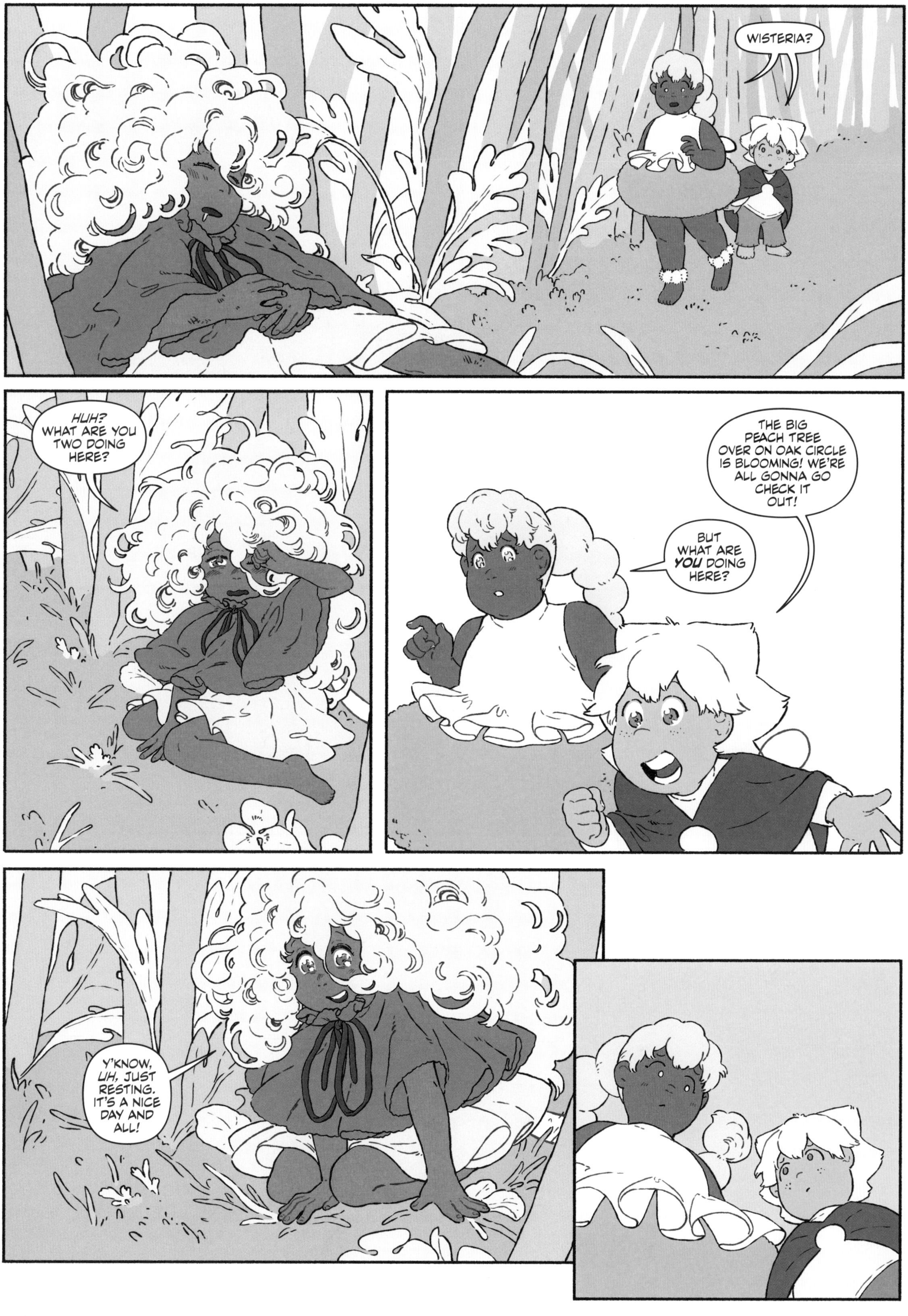
WISTERIA?
HUH? WHAT ARE YOU TWO DOING HERE?
THE BIG PEACH TREE OVER ON OAK CIRCLE IS BLOOMING! WE'RE ALL GONNA GO CHECK IT OUT!
BUT WHAT ARE YOU DOING HERE?
Y'KNOW, UH, JUST RESTING. IT'S A NICE DAY AND ALL!

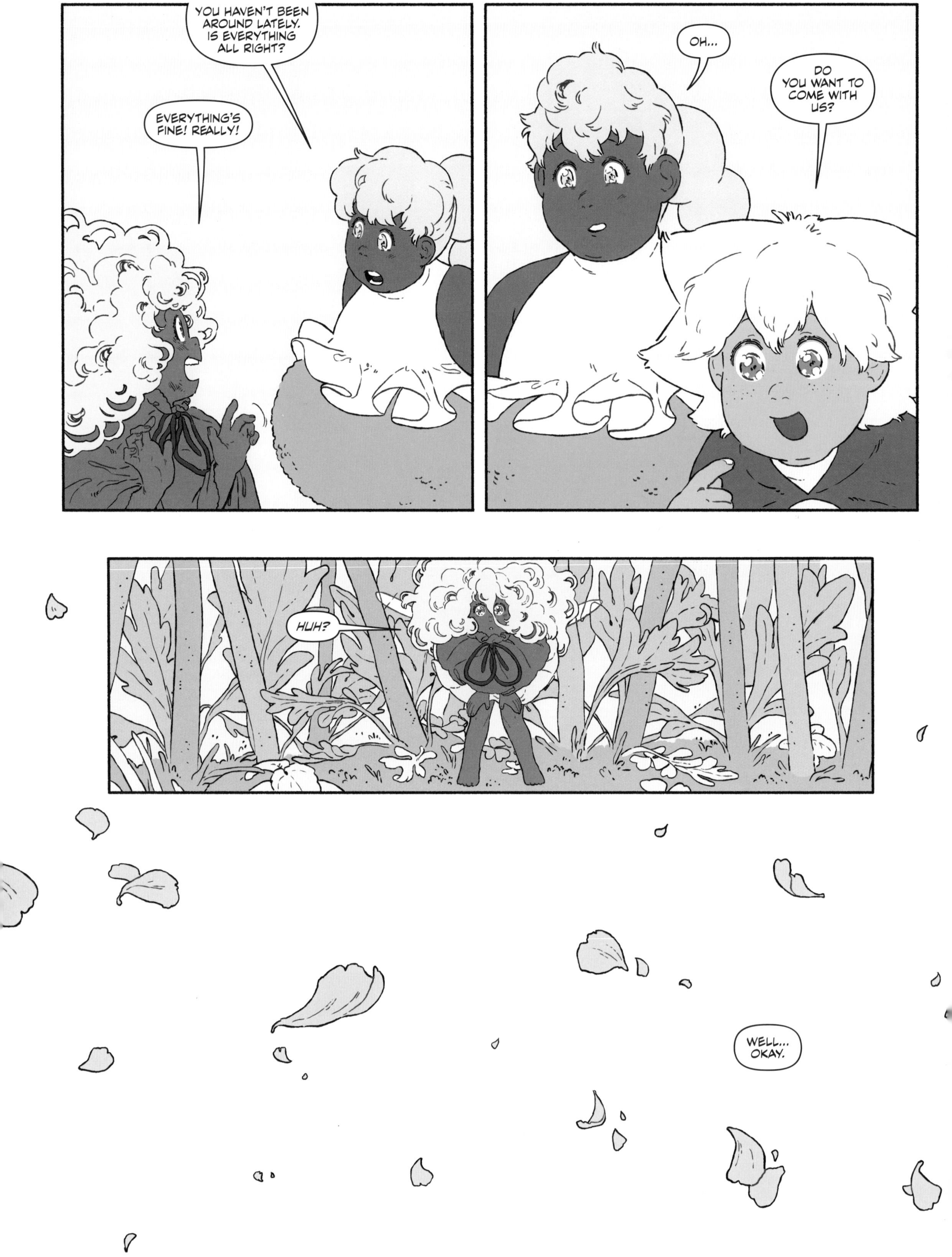
YOU HAVEN'T BEEN AROUND LATELY. IS EVERYTHING ALL RIGHT?
EVERYTHING'S FINE! REALLY!
OH...
DO YOU WANT TO COME WITH US?
HUH?
WELL... OKAY.

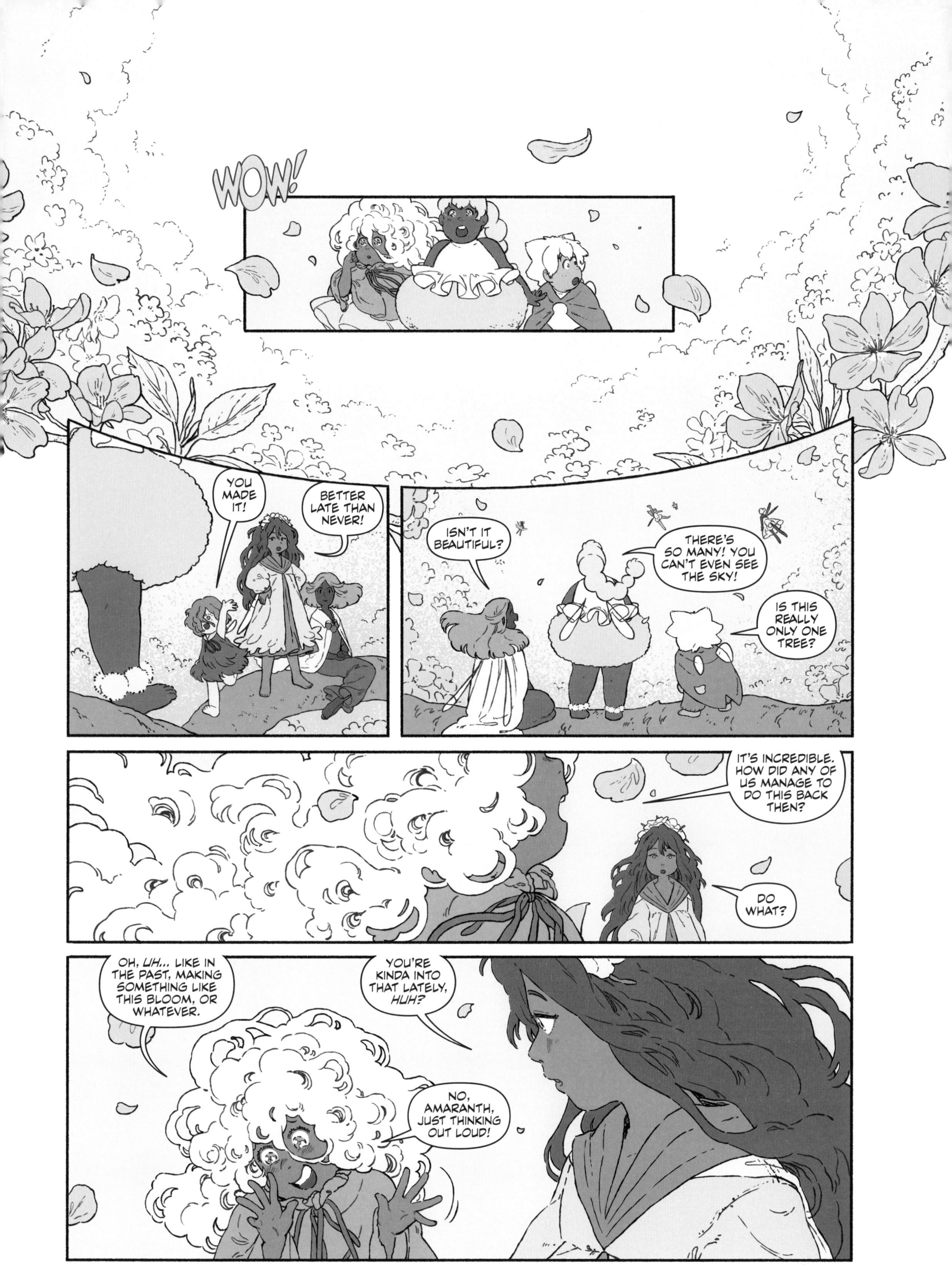
WOW!
YOU MADE IT!
BETTER LATE THAN NEVER!
ISN'T IT BEAUTIFUL?
THERE'S SO MANY! YOU CAN'T EVEN SEE THE SKY!
IS THIS REALLY ONLY ONE TREE?
IT'S INCREDIBLE. HOW DID ANY OF US MANAGE TO DO THIS BACK THEN?
DO WHAT?
OH, *UH*... LIKE IN THE PAST, MAKING SOMETHING LIKE THIS BLOOM, OR WHATEVER.
YOU'RE KINDA INTO THAT LATELY, *HUH?*
NO, AMARANTH, JUST THINKING OUT LOUD!

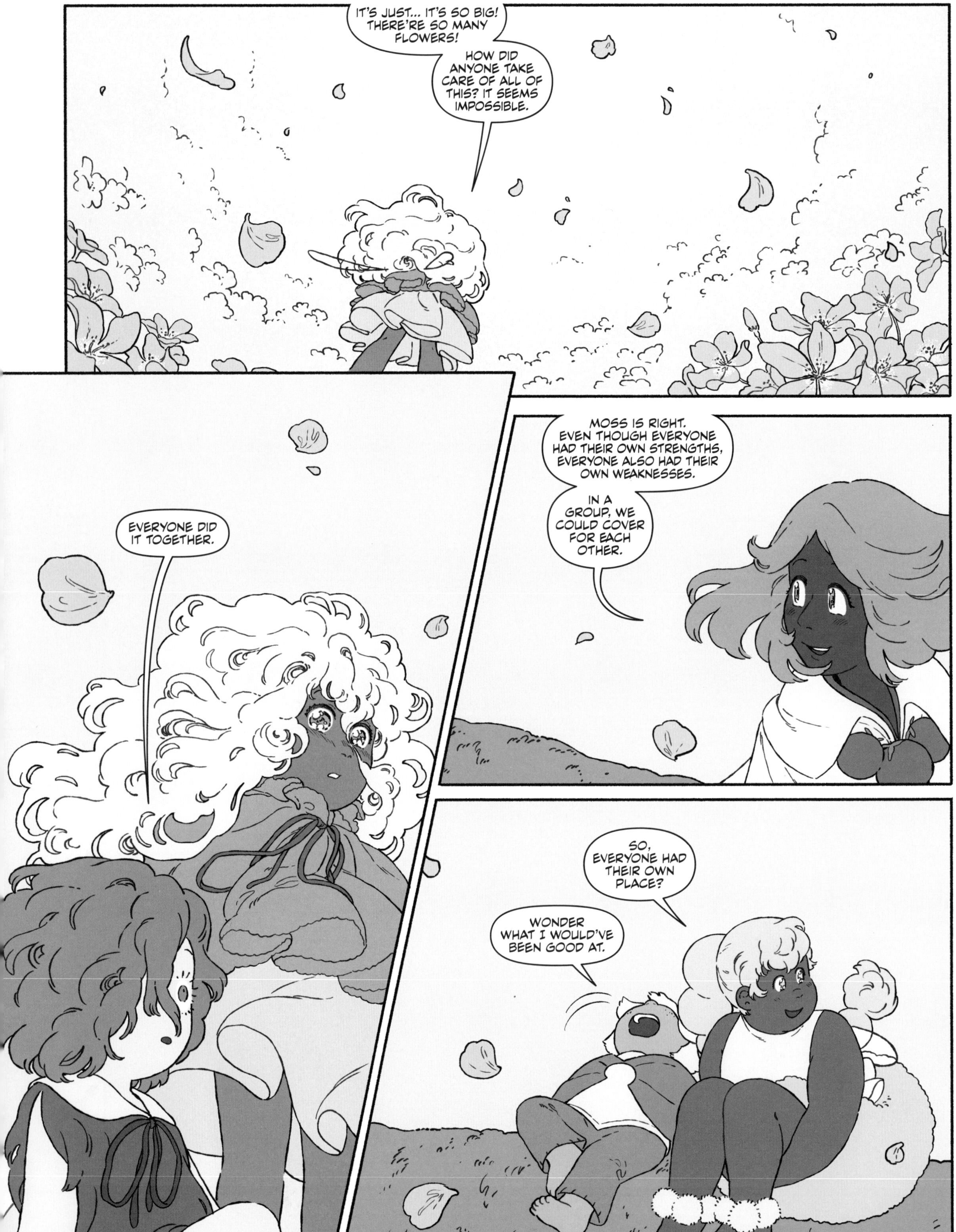

IT'S JUST... IT'S SO BIG! THERE'RE SO MANY FLOWERS!
HOW DID ANYONE TAKE CARE OF ALL OF THIS? IT SEEMS IMPOSSIBLE.
EVERYONE DID IT TOGETHER.
MOSS IS RIGHT. EVEN THOUGH EVERYONE HAD THEIR OWN STRENGTHS, EVERYONE ALSO HAD THEIR OWN WEAKNESSES.
IN A GROUP, WE COULD COVER FOR EACH OTHER.
SO, EVERYONE HAD THEIR OWN PLACE?
WONDER WHAT I WOULD'VE BEEN GOOD AT.

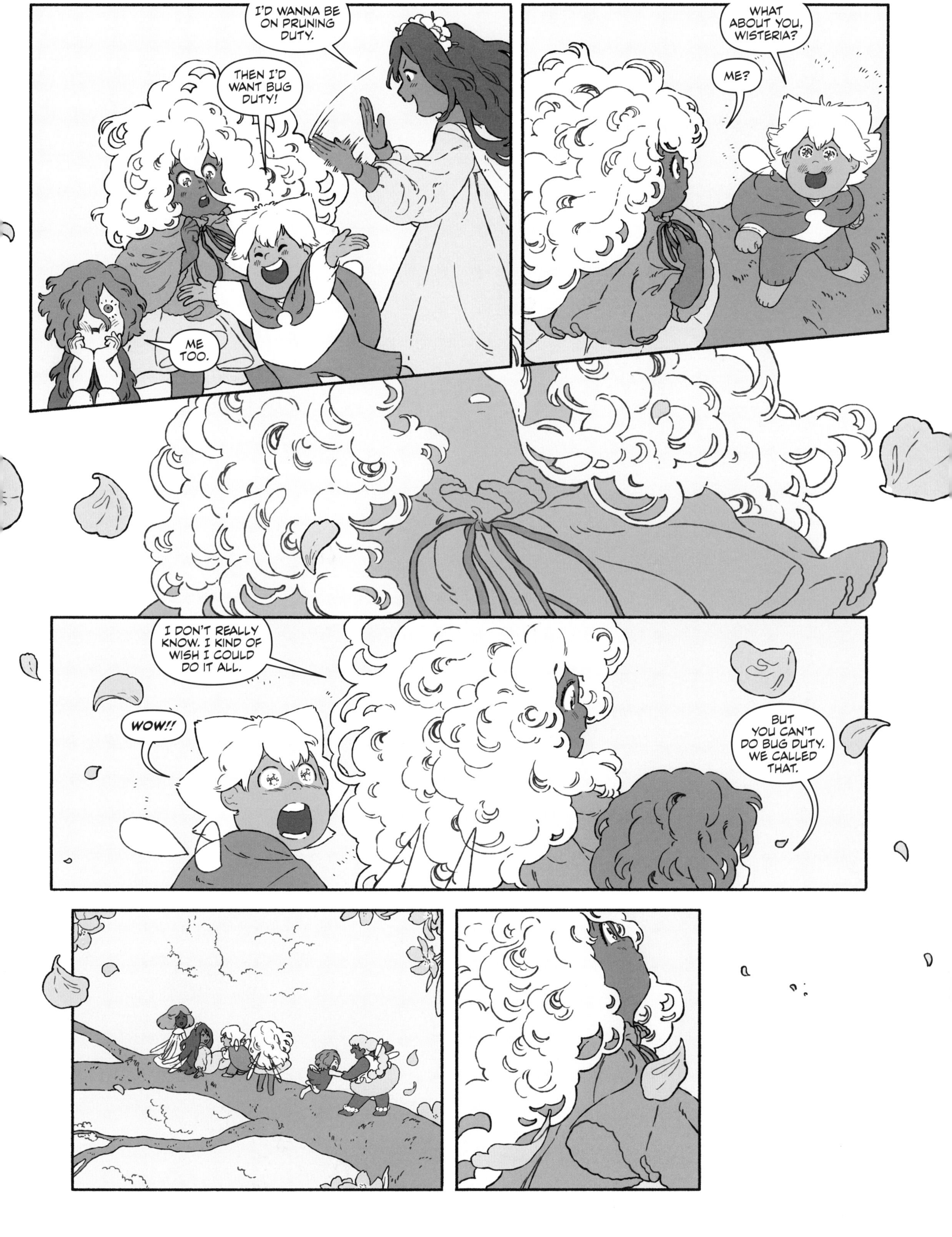
I'D WANNA BE ON PRUNING DUTY.
THEN I'D WANT BUG DUTY!
ME TOO.
WHAT ABOUT YOU, WISTERIA?
ME?
I DON'T REALLY KNOW. I KIND OF WISH I COULD DO IT ALL.
WOW!!
BUT YOU CAN'T DO BUG DUTY. WE CALLED THAT.

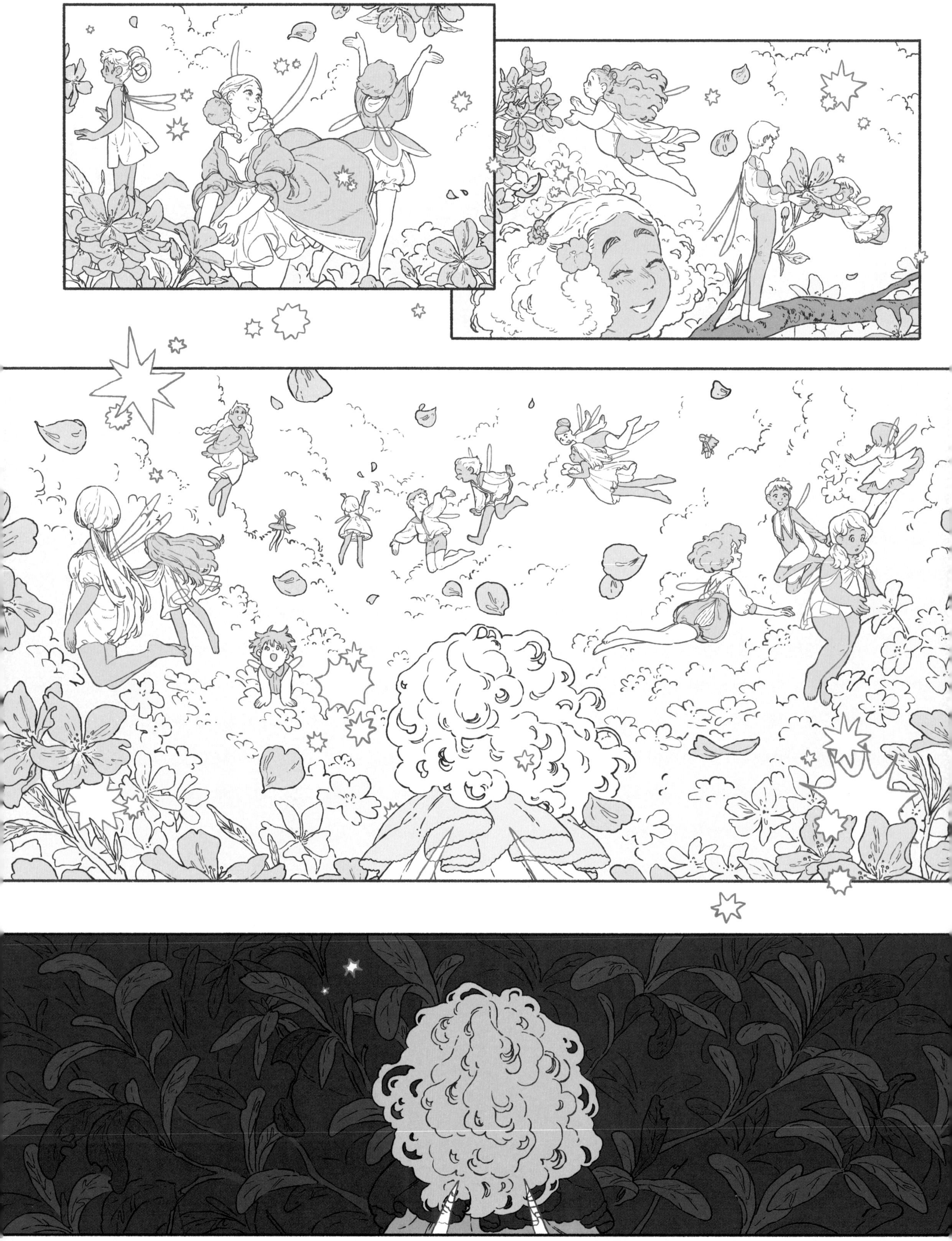

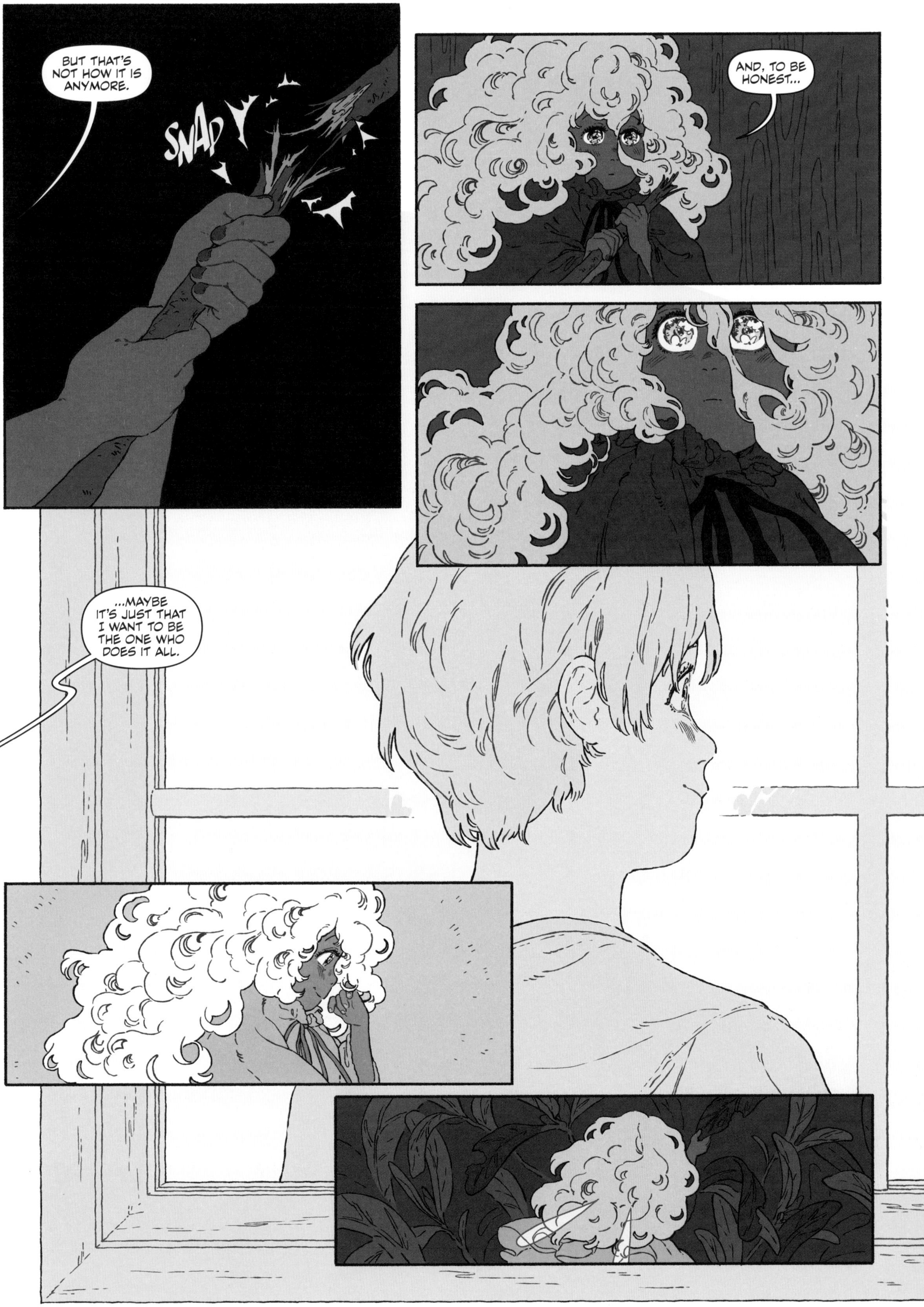
BUT THAT'S NOT HOW IT IS ANYMORE.
SNAP
AND, TO BE HONEST...
...MAYBE IT'S JUST THAT I WANT TO BE THE ONE WHO DOES IT ALL.

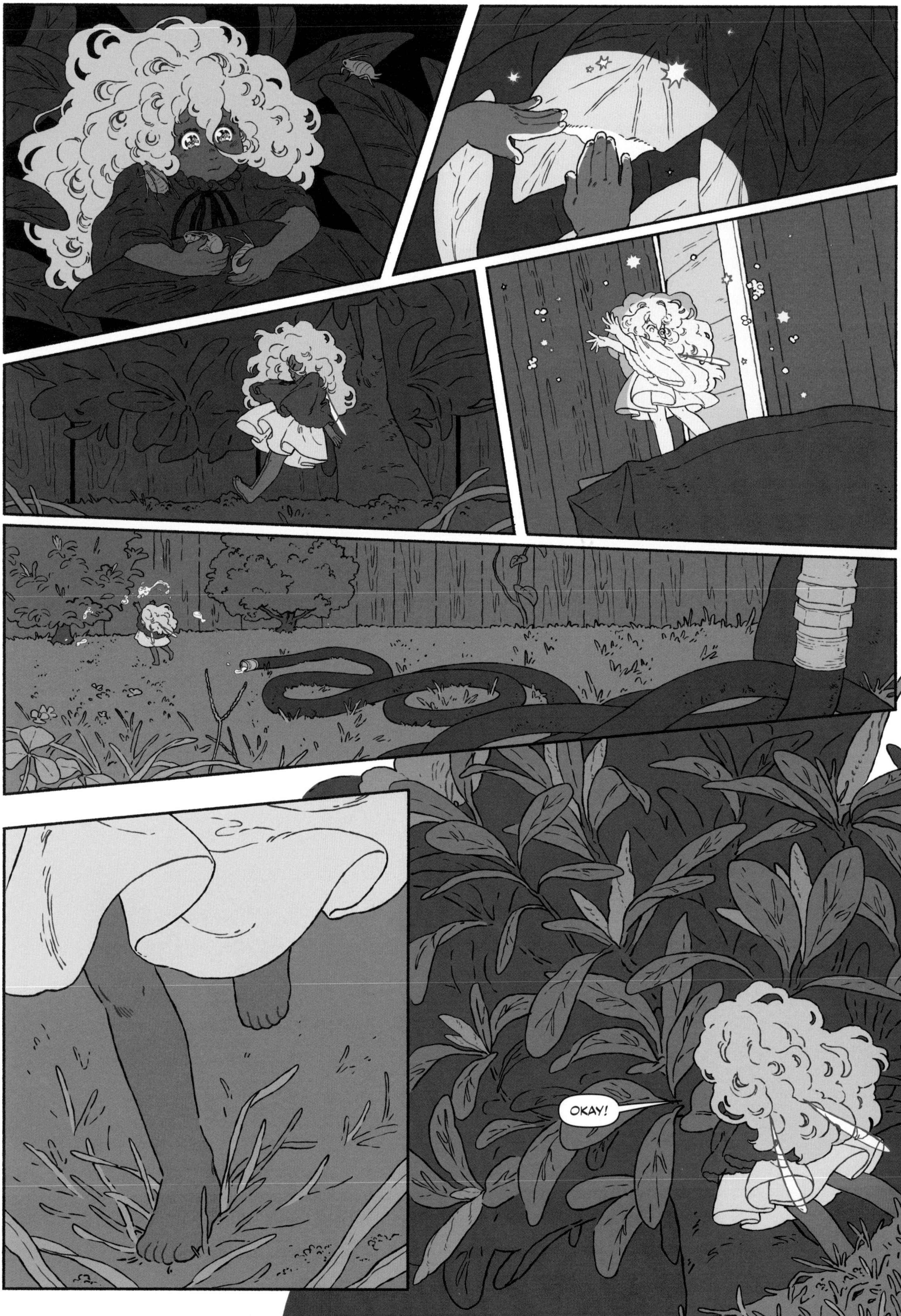
OKAY!

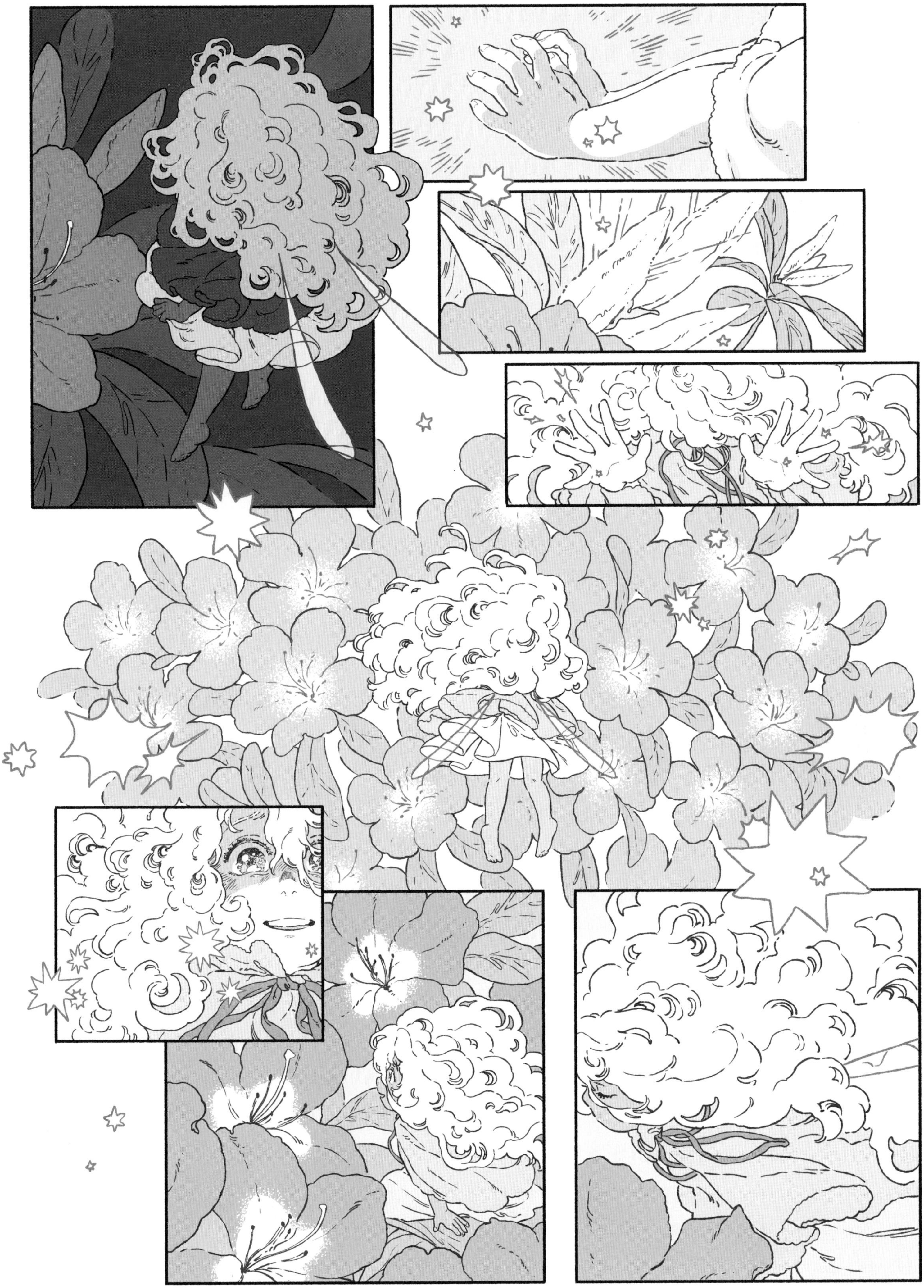

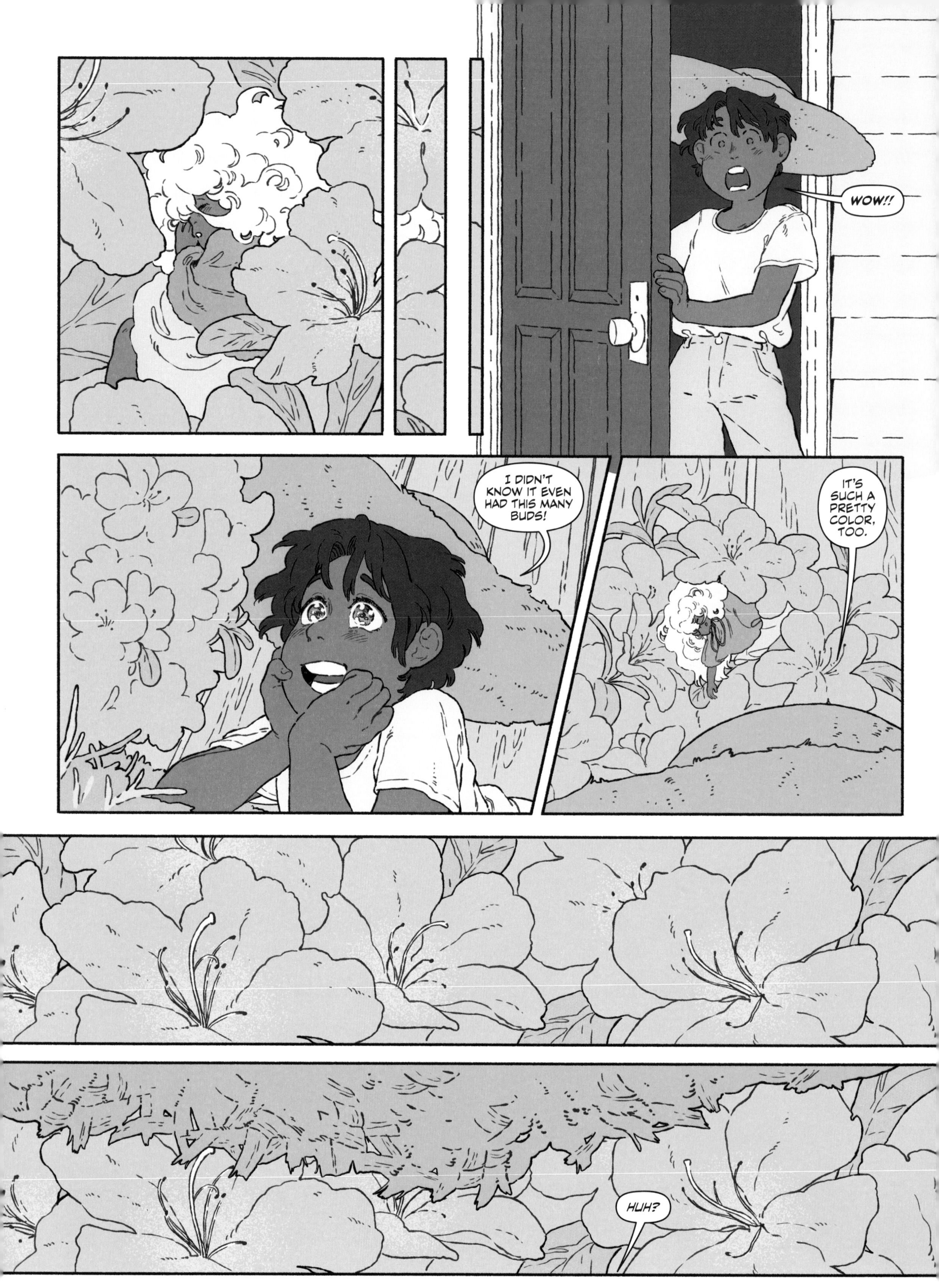
WOW!!
I DIDN'T KNOW IT EVEN HAD THIS MANY BUDS!
IT'S SUCH A PRETTY COLOR, TOO.
HUH?

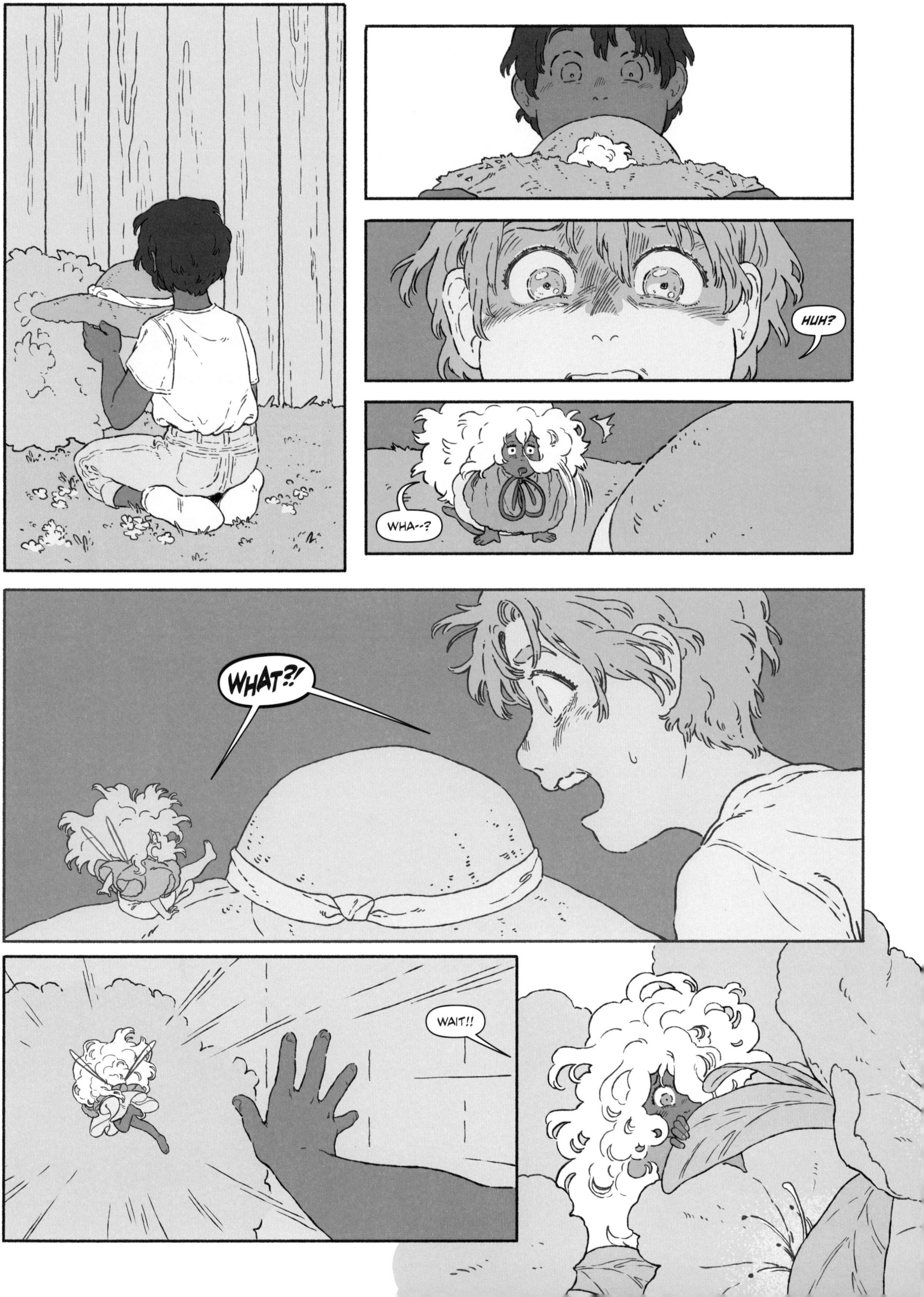
HUH?
WHA--?
WHAT?!
WAIT!!

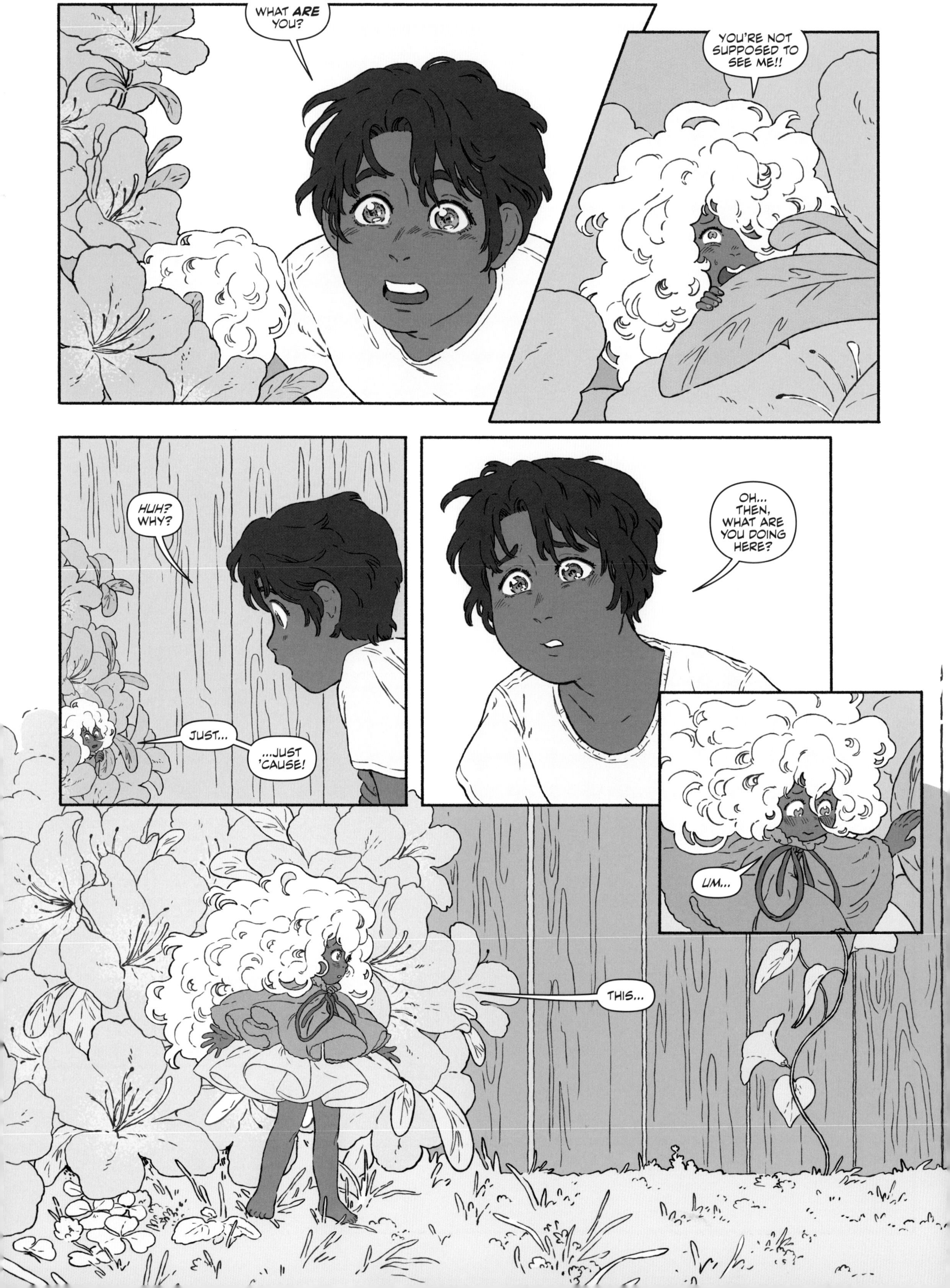

WHAT ARE YOU?
YOU'RE NOT SUPPOSED TO SEE ME!!
HUH? WHY?
JUST...
...JUST 'CAUSE!
OH... THEN, WHAT ARE YOU DOING HERE?
UM...
THIS...

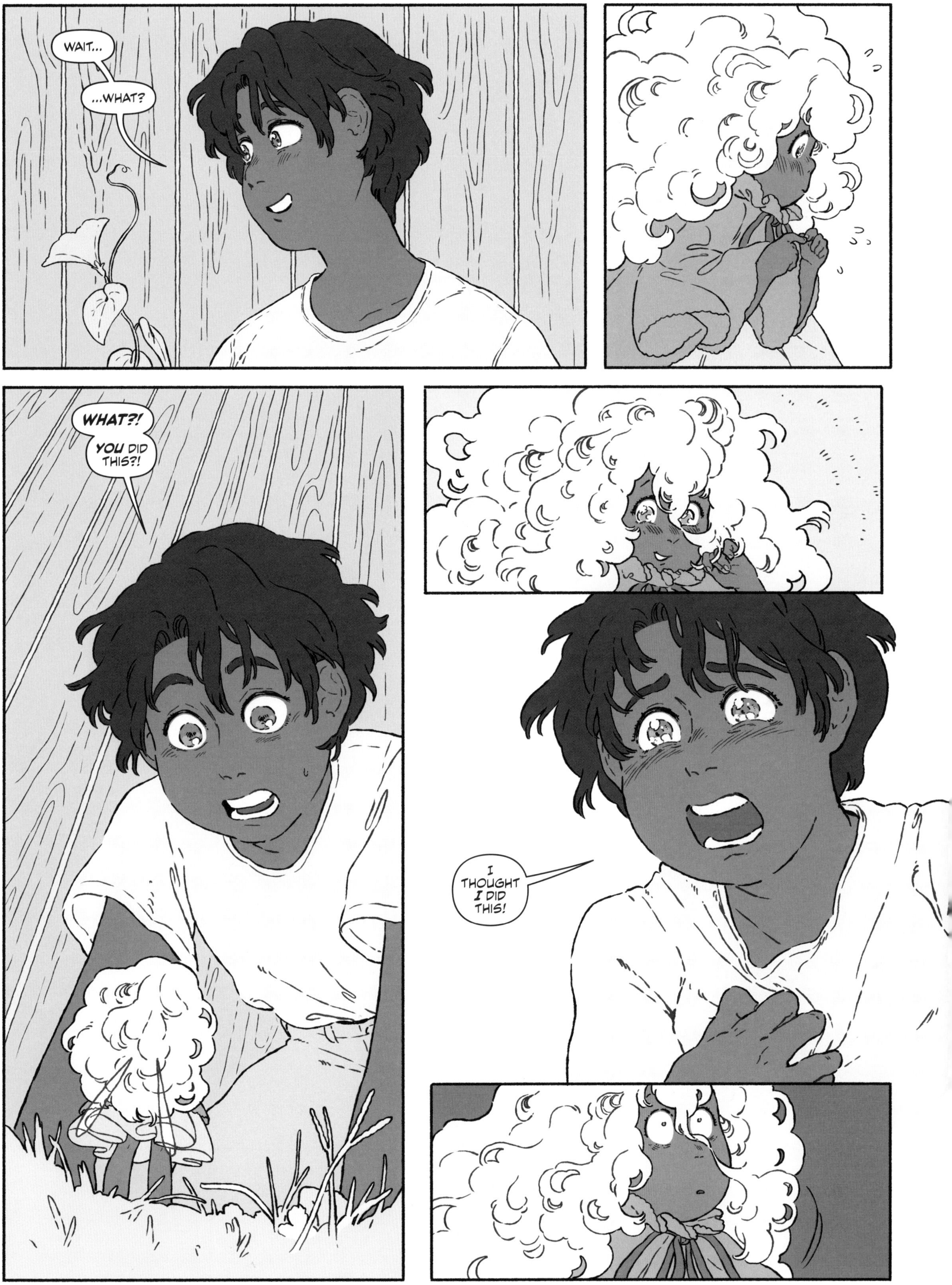
WAIT...
...WHAT?
WHAT?!
YOU DID THIS?!
I THOUGHT I DID THIS!

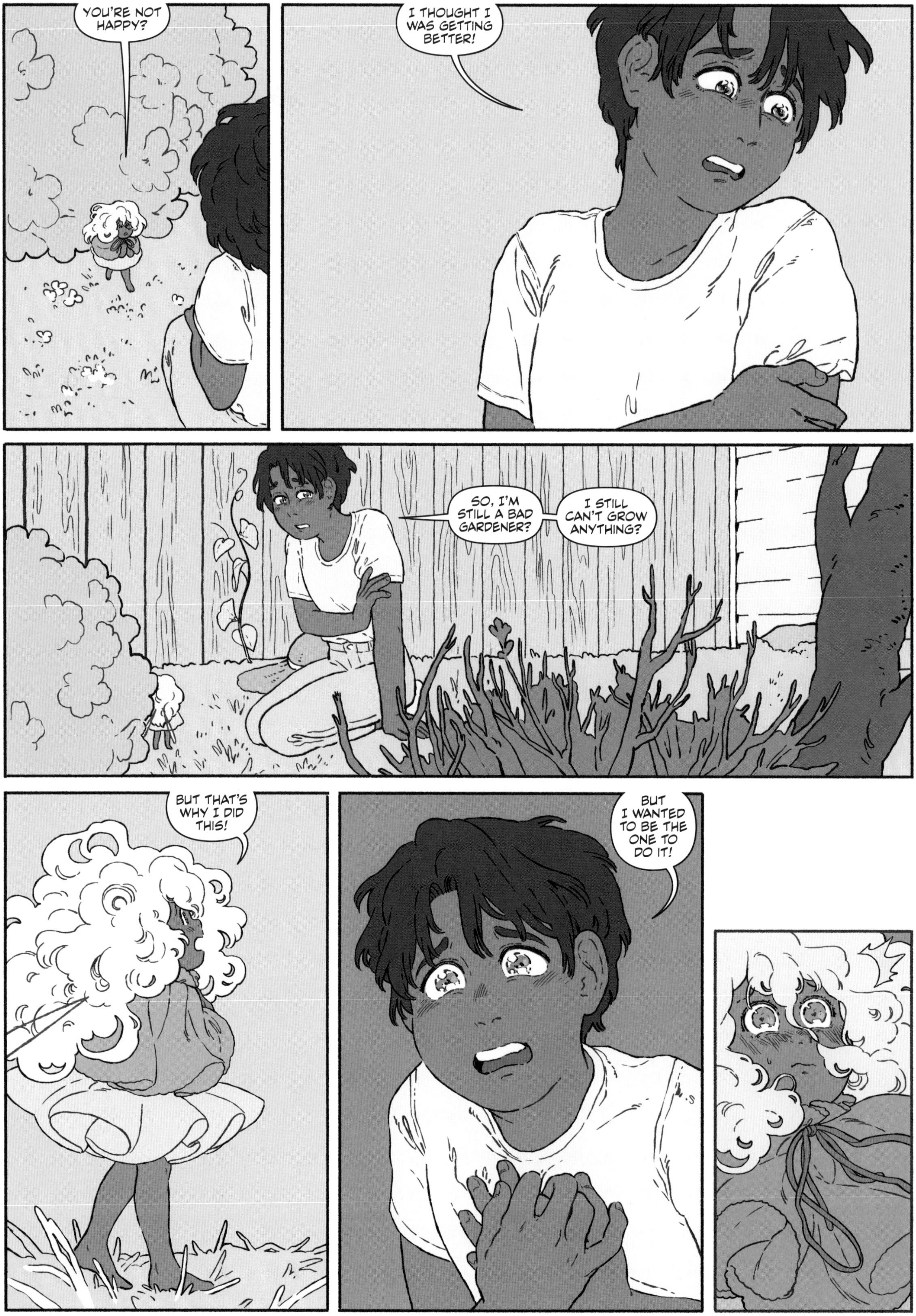
YOU'RE NOT HAPPY?
I THOUGHT I WAS GETTING BETTER!
SO, I'M STILL A BAD GARDENER?
I STILL CAN'T GROW ANYTHING?
BUT THAT'S WHY I DID THIS!
BUT I WANTED TO BE THE ONE TO DO IT!

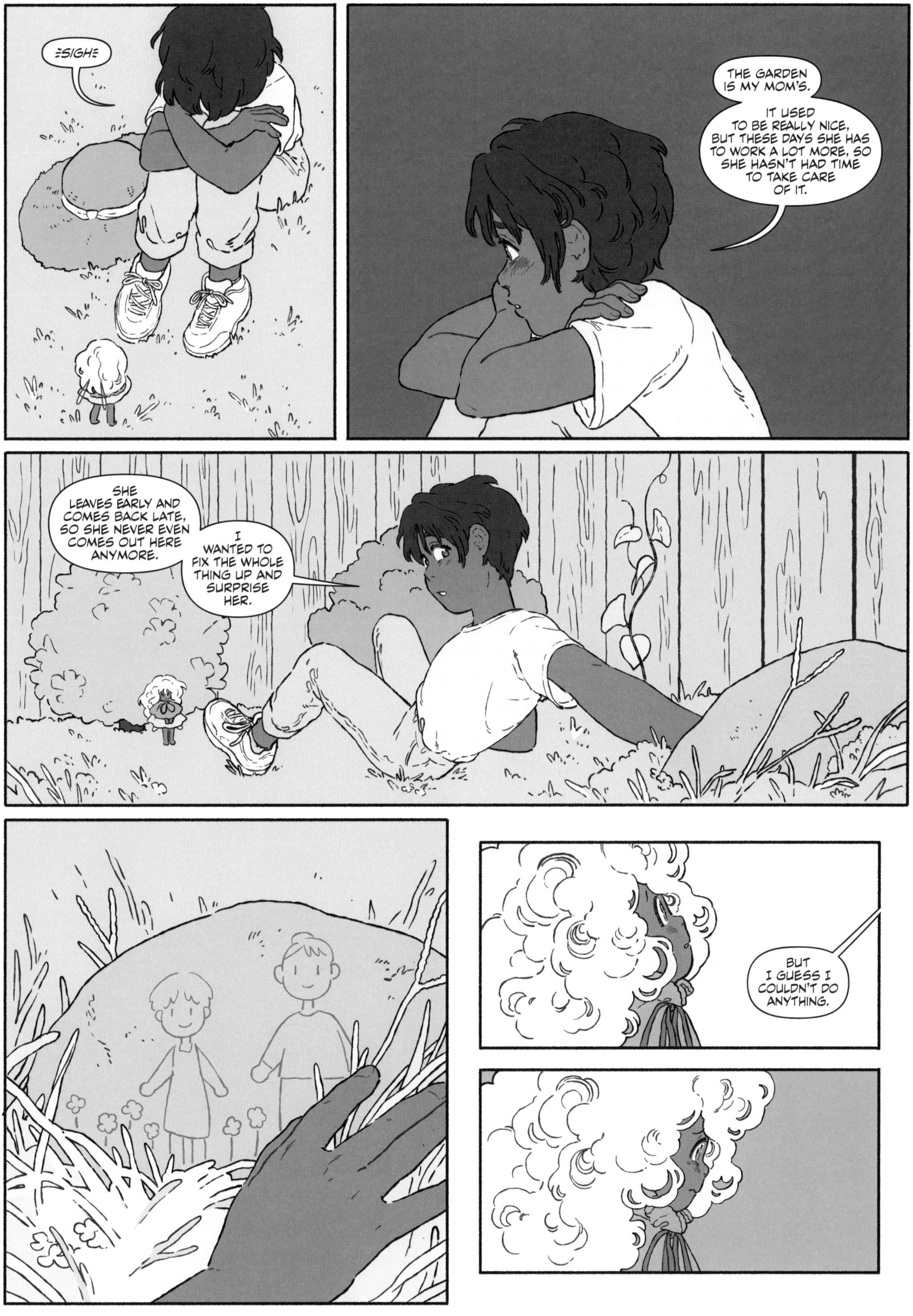

SIGH
THE GARDEN IS MY MOM'S.
IT USED TO BE REALLY NICE, BUT THESE DAYS SHE HAS TO WORK A LOT MORE, SO SHE HASN'T HAD TIME TO TAKE CARE OF IT.
SHE LEAVES EARLY AND COMES BACK LATE, SO SHE NEVER EVEN COMES OUT HERE ANYMORE.
I WANTED TO FIX THE WHOLE THING UP AND SURPRISE HER.
BUT I GUESS I COULDN'T DO ANYTHING.

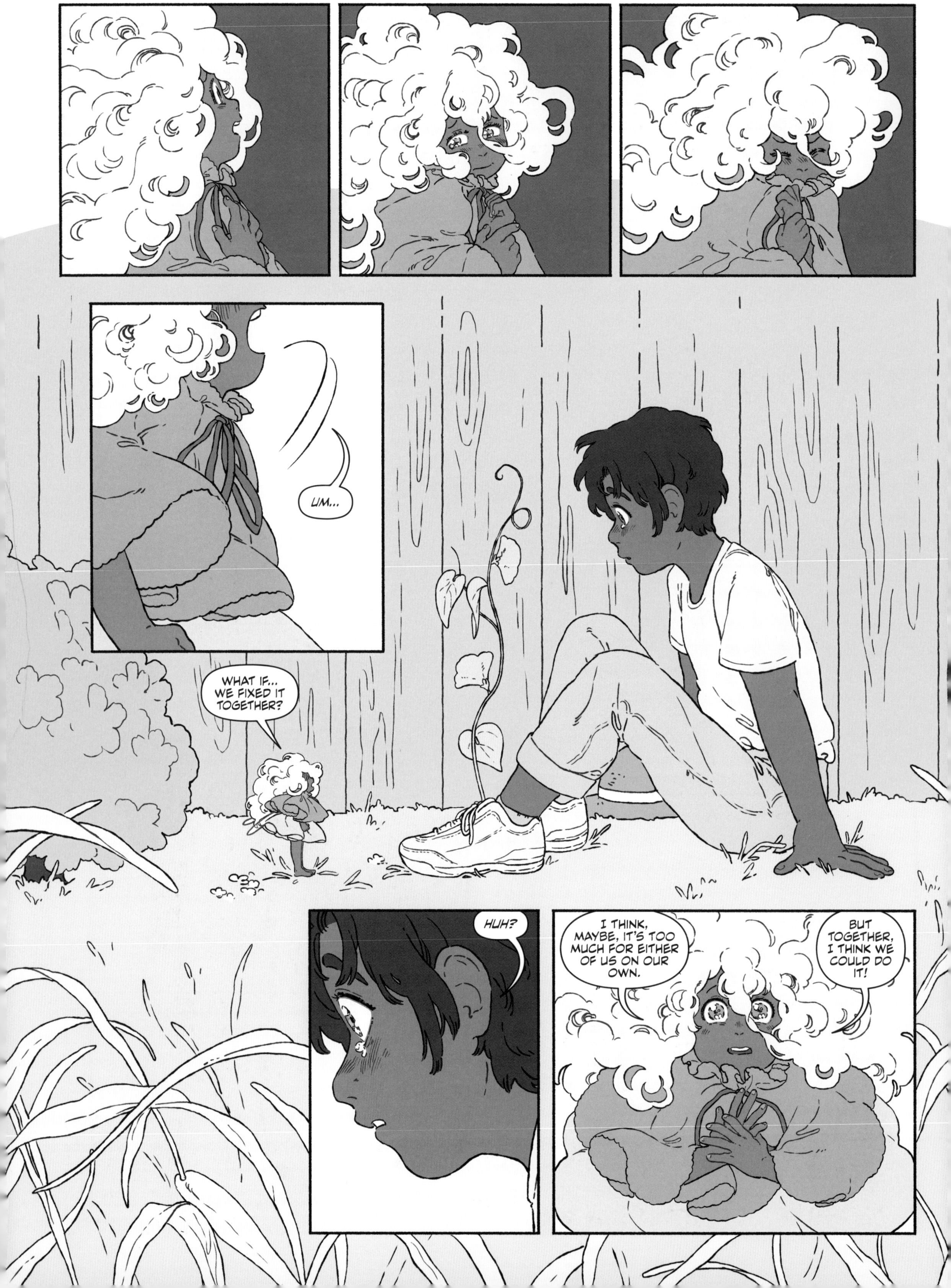
UM...
WHAT IF... WE FIXED IT TOGETHER?
HUH?
I THINK, MAYBE, IT'S TOO MUCH FOR EITHER OF US ON OUR OWN.
BUT TOGETHER, I THINK WE COULD DO IT!

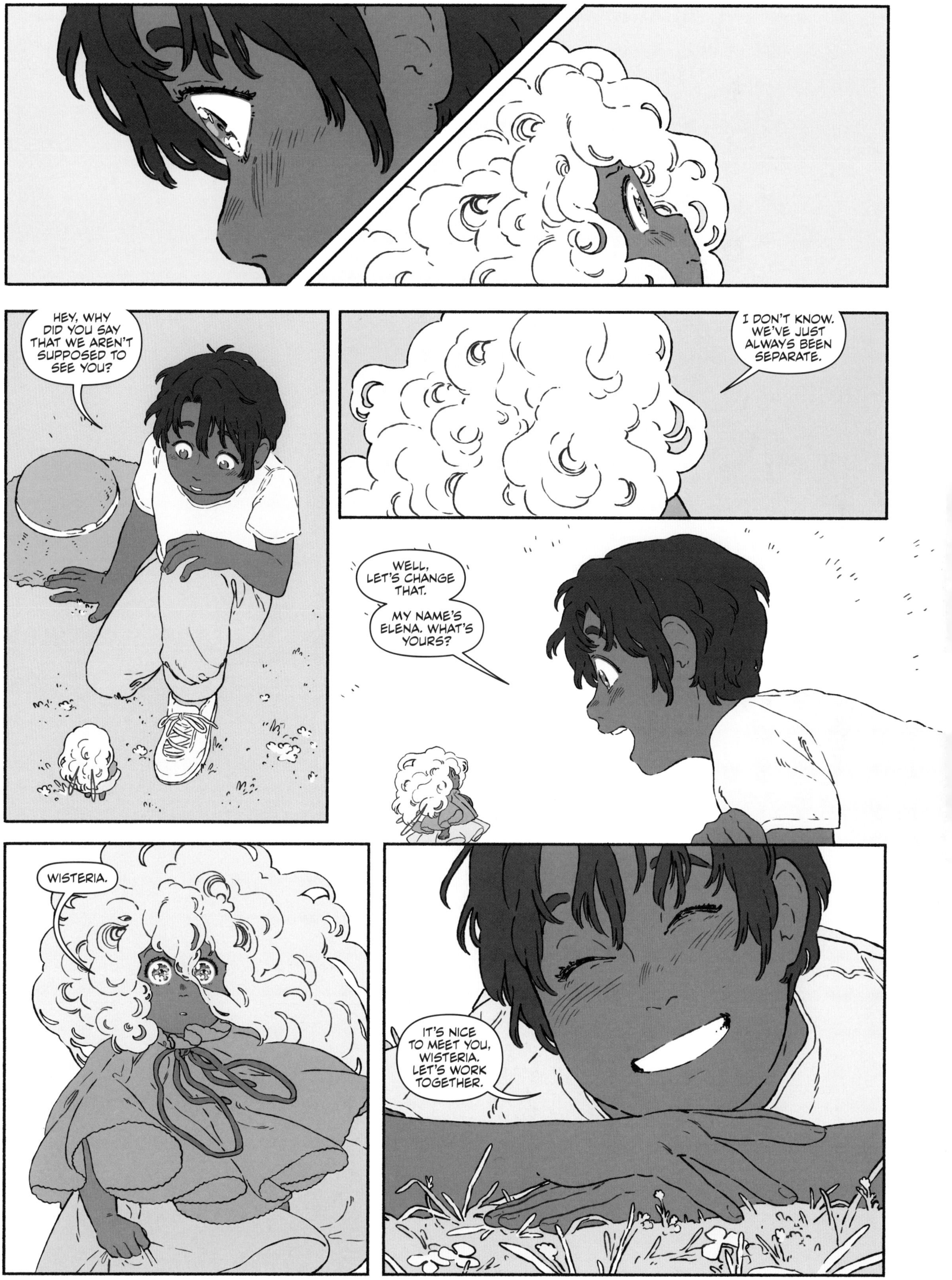
HEY, WHY DID YOU SAY THAT WE AREN'T SUPPOSED TO SEE YOU?
I DON'T KNOW. WE'VE JUST ALWAYS BEEN SEPARATE.
WELL, LET'S CHANGE THAT.
MY NAME'S ELENA. WHAT'S YOURS?
WISTERIA.
IT'S NICE TO MEET YOU, WISTERIA. LET'S WORK TOGETHER.

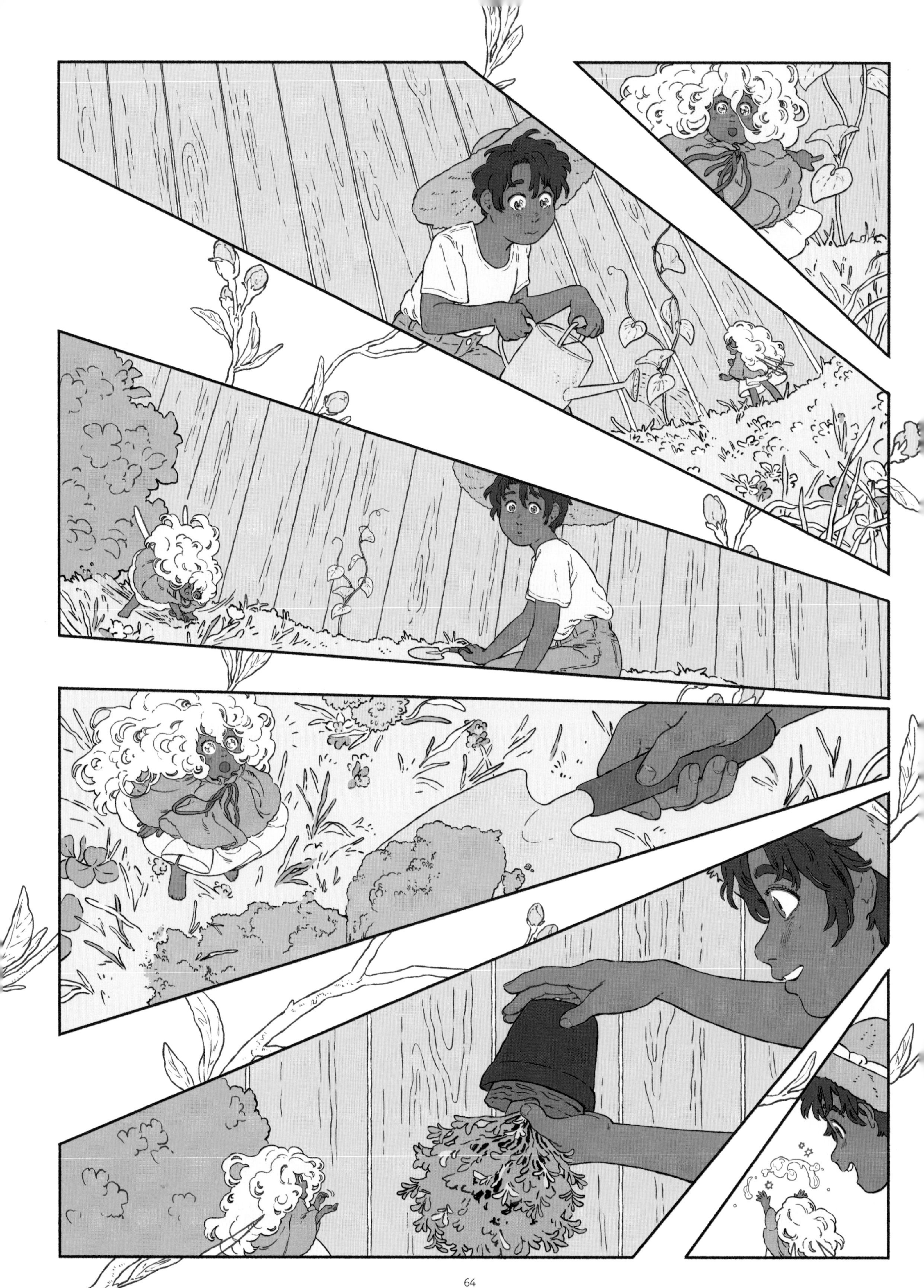

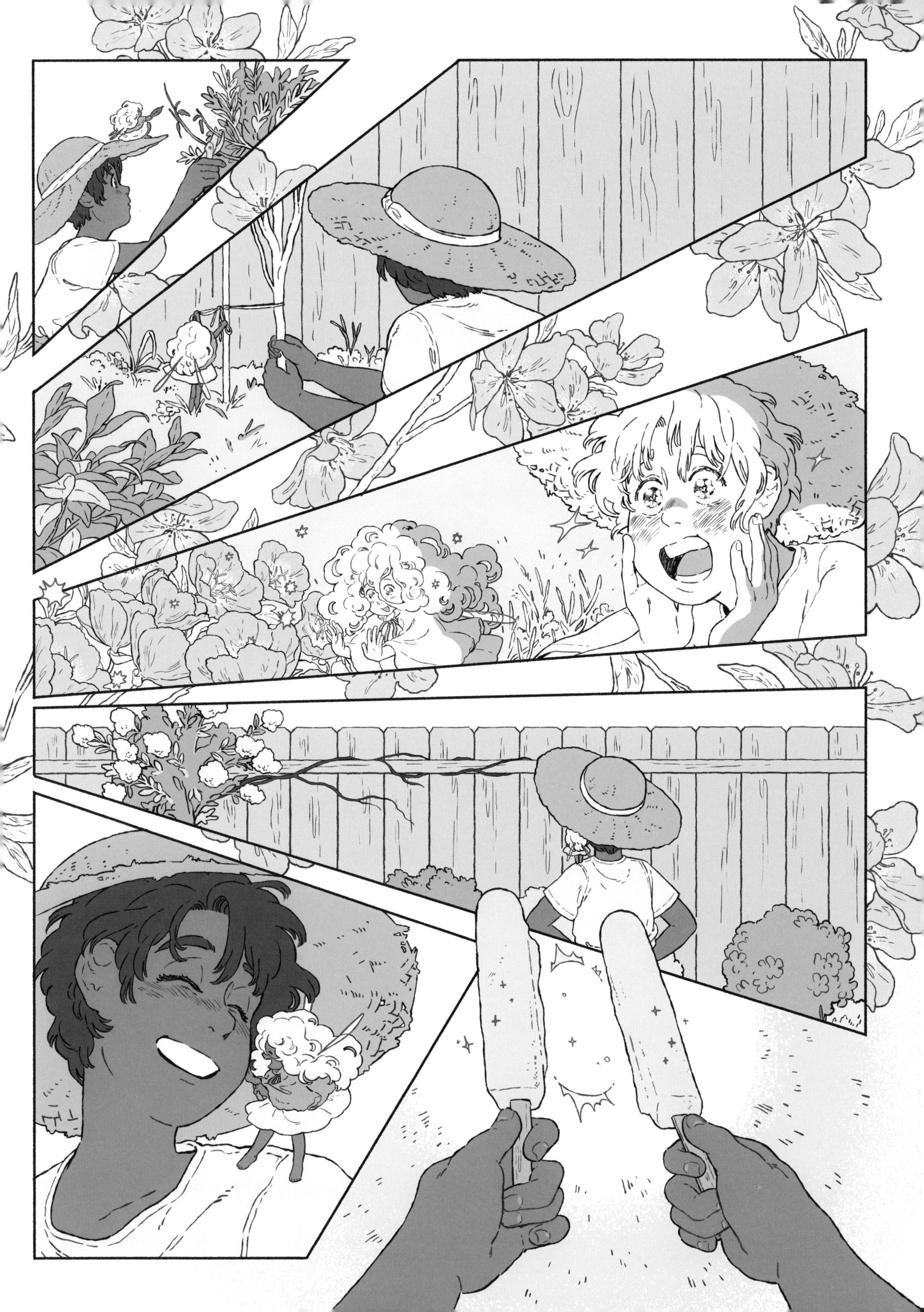

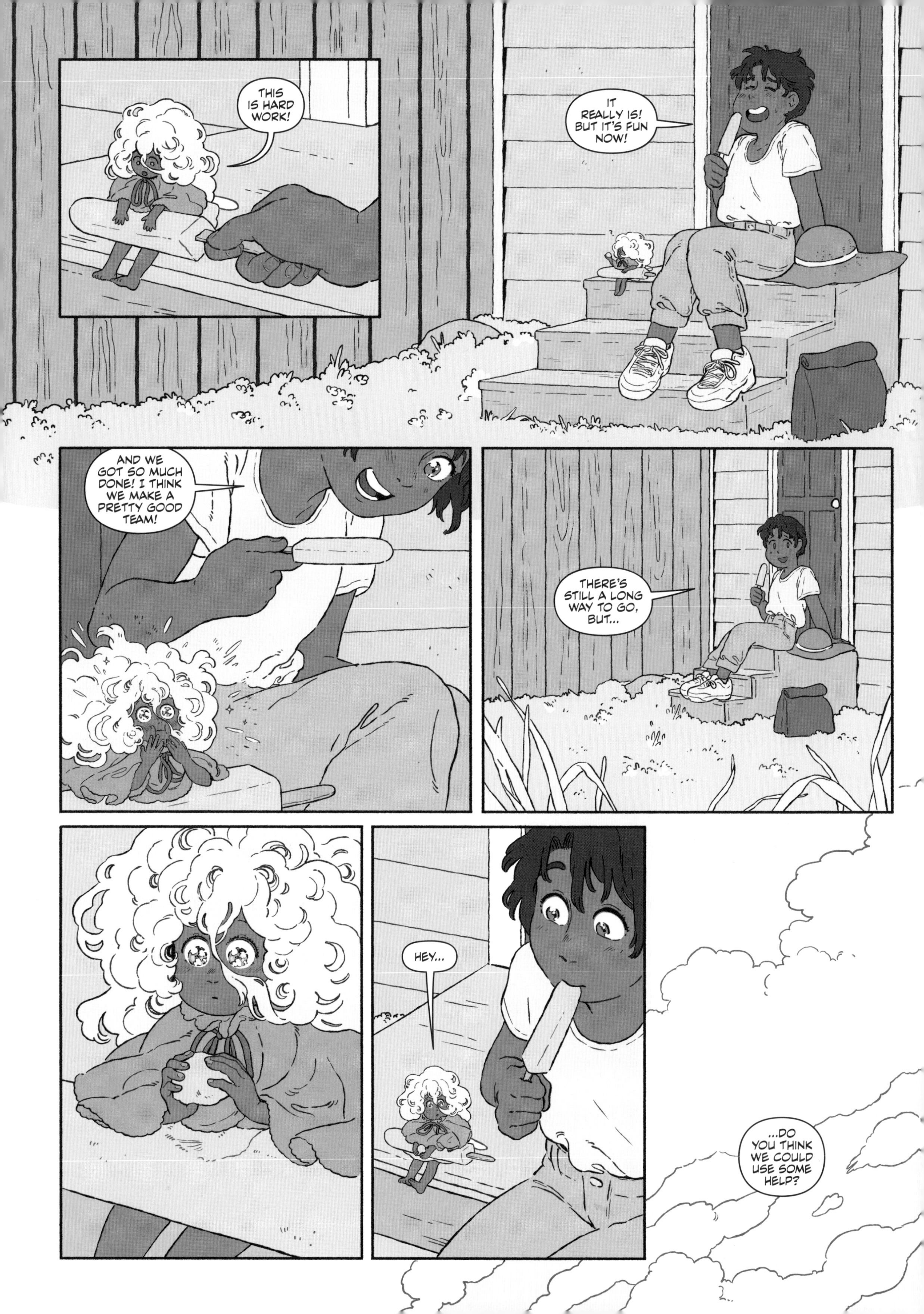
THIS IS HARD WORK!
IT REALLY IS! BUT IT'S FUN NOW!
AND WE GOT SO MUCH DONE! I THINK WE MAKE A PRETTY GOOD TEAM!
THERE'S STILL A LONG WAY TO GO, BUT...
HEY...
...DO YOU THINK WE COULD USE SOME HELP?

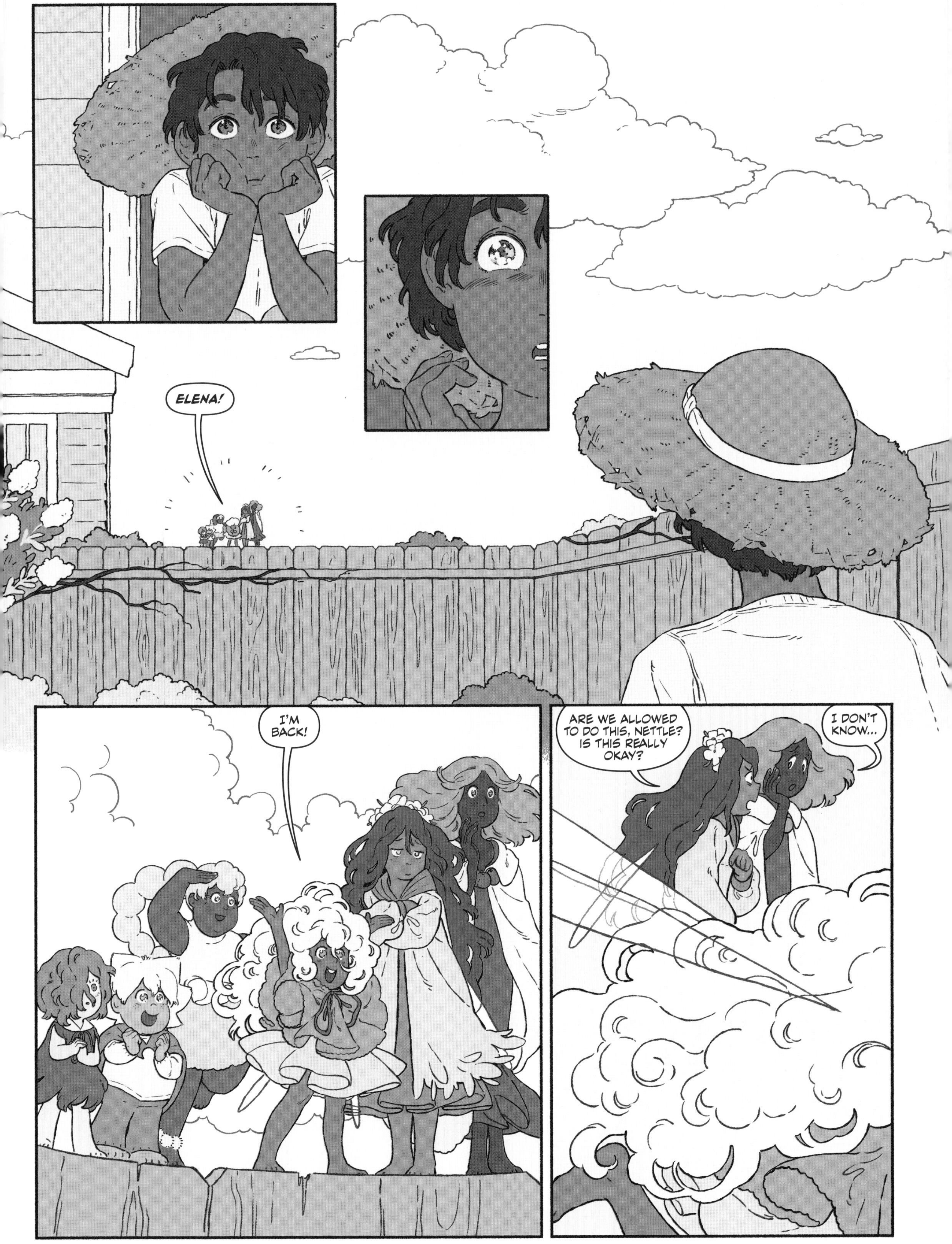
ELENA!
I'M BACK!
ARE WE ALLOWED TO DO THIS, NETTLE? IS THIS REALLY OKAY?
I DON'T KNOW...

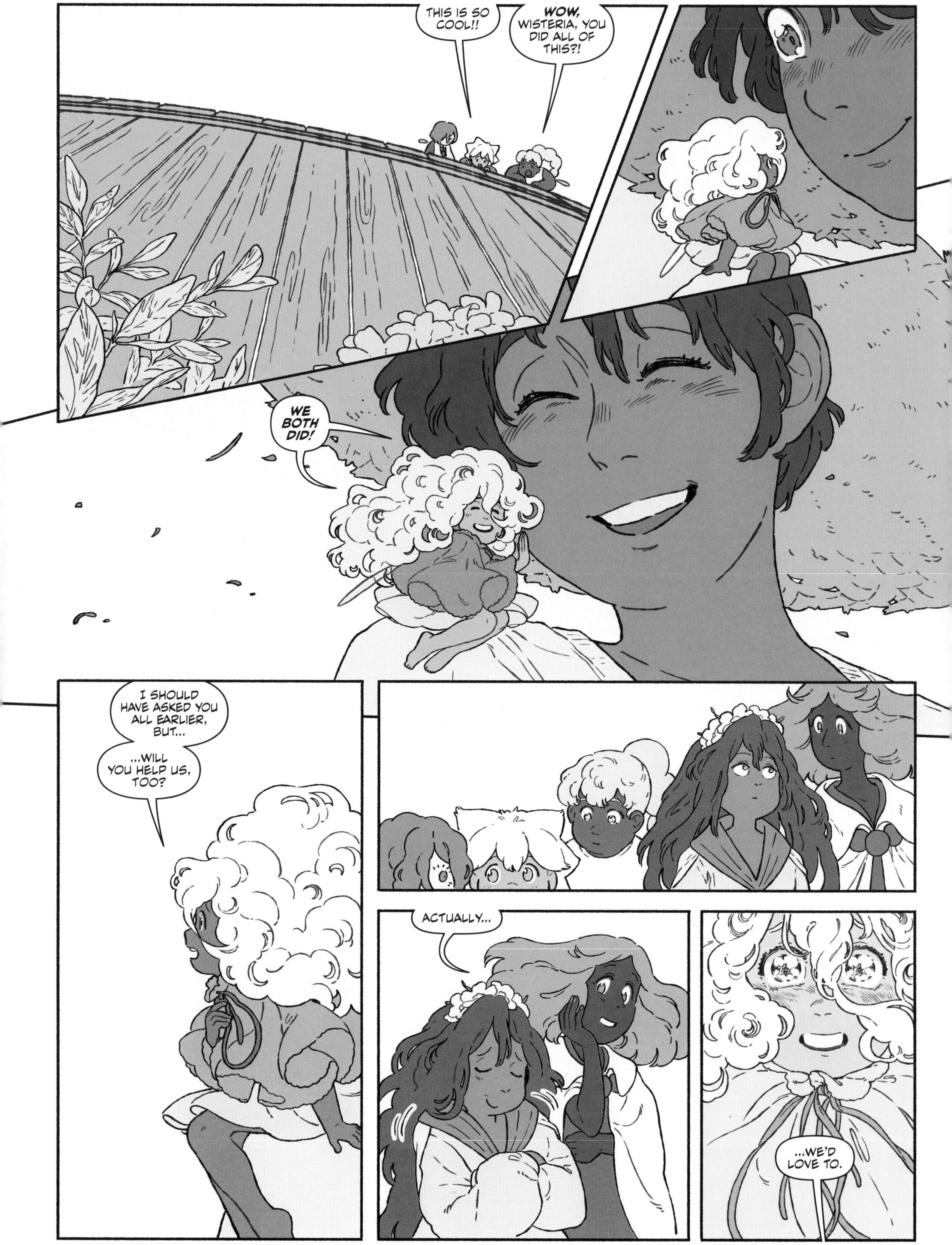
THIS IS SO COOL!!
WOW, WISTERIA, YOU DID ALL OF THIS?!
WE BOTH DID!
I SHOULD HAVE ASKED YOU ALL EARLIER, BUT...
...WILL YOU HELP US, TOO?
ACTUALLY...
...WE'D LOVE TO.

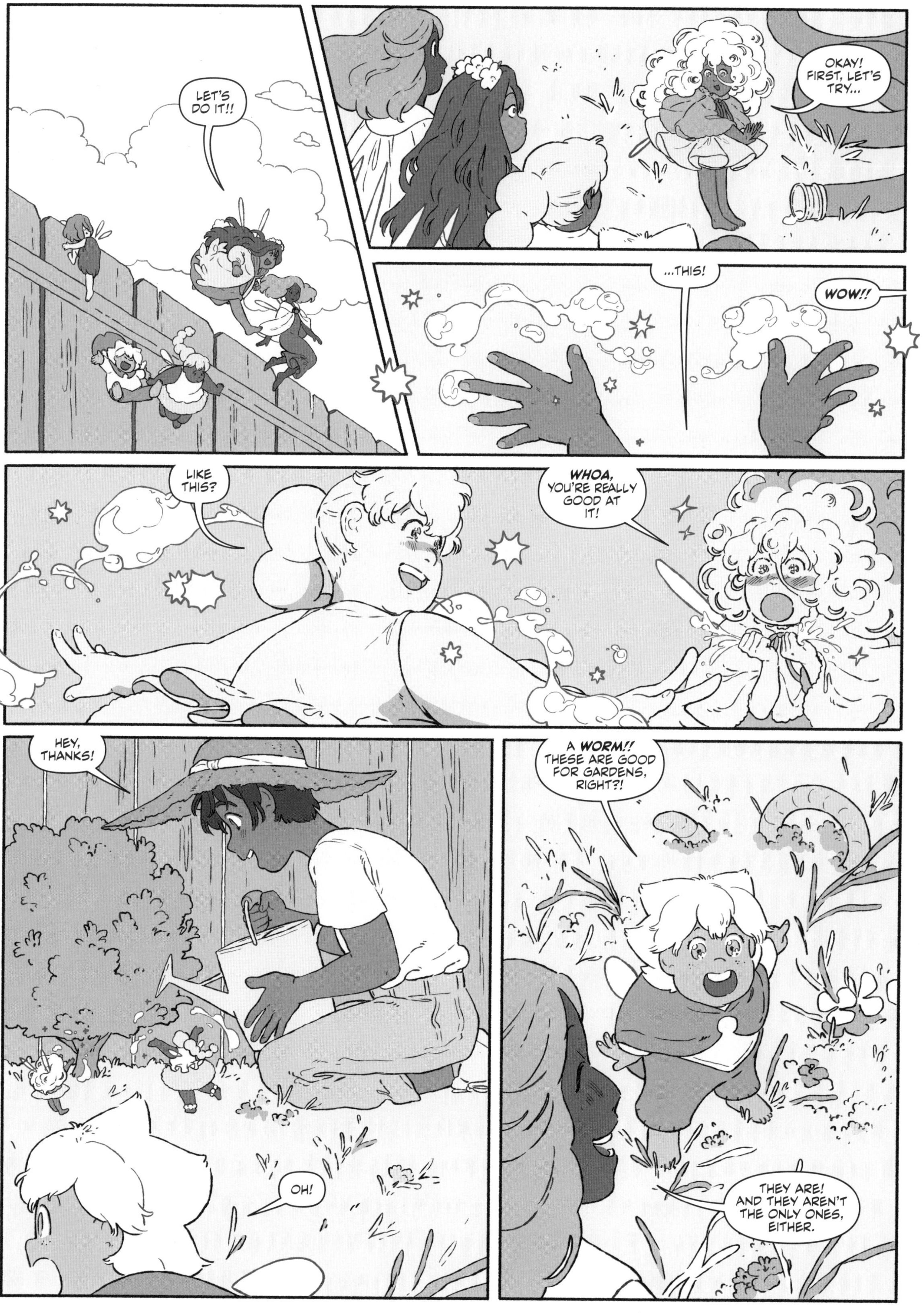
LET'S DO IT!!
OKAY! FIRST, LET'S TRY...
...THIS!
WOW!!
LIKE THIS?
WHOA, YOU'RE REALLY GOOD AT IT!
HEY, THANKS!
OH!
A WORM!! THESE ARE GOOD FOR GARDENS, RIGHT?!
THEY ARE! AND THEY AREN'T THE ONLY ONES, EITHER.

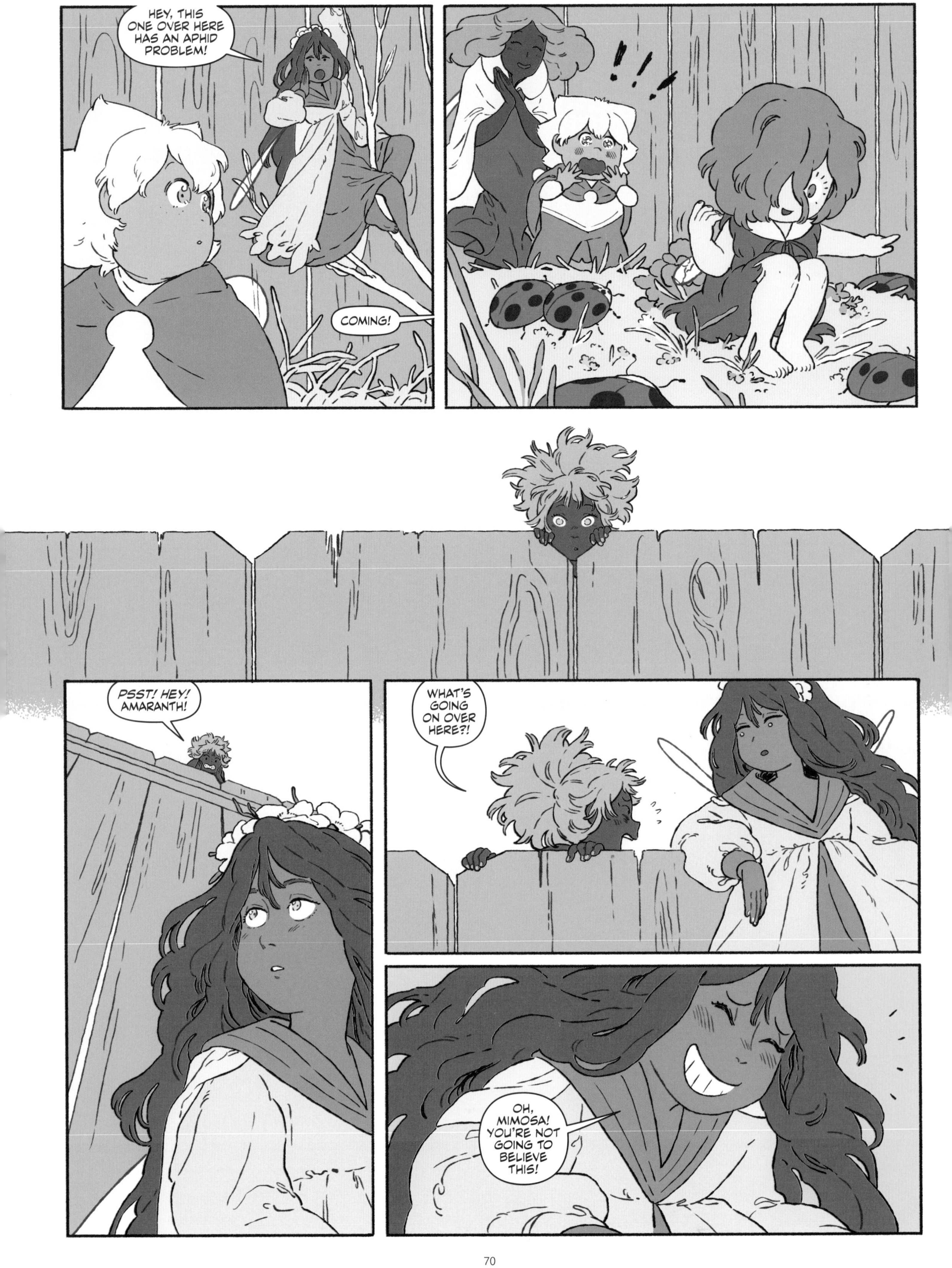

HEY, THIS ONE OVER HERE HAS AN APHID PROBLEM!
COMING!
!!!
PSST! HEY! AMARANTH!
WHAT'S GOING ON OVER HERE?!
OH, MIMOSA! YOU'RE NOT GOING TO BELIEVE THIS!

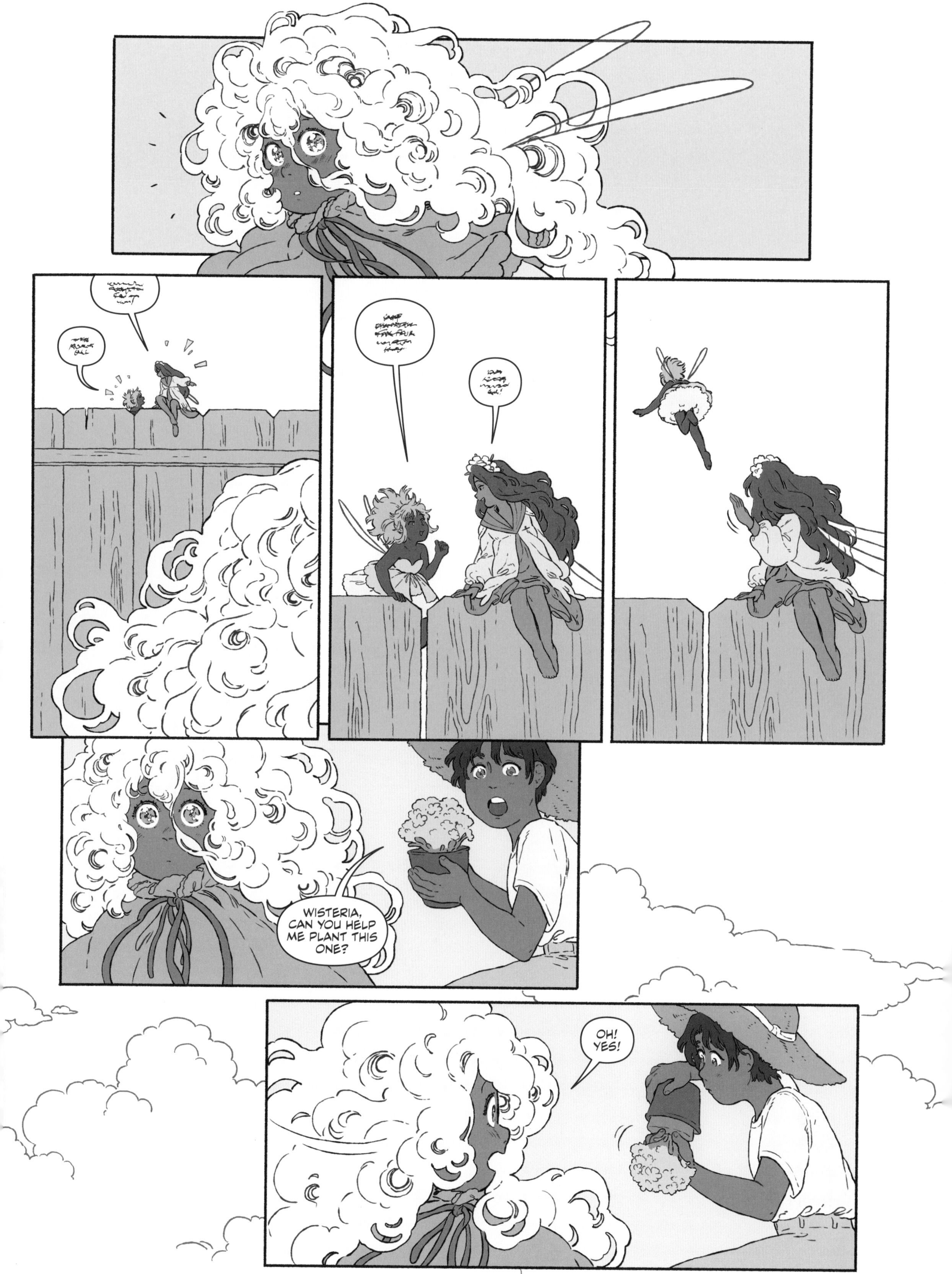
WISTERIA, CAN YOU HELP ME PLANT THIS ONE?
OH! YES!

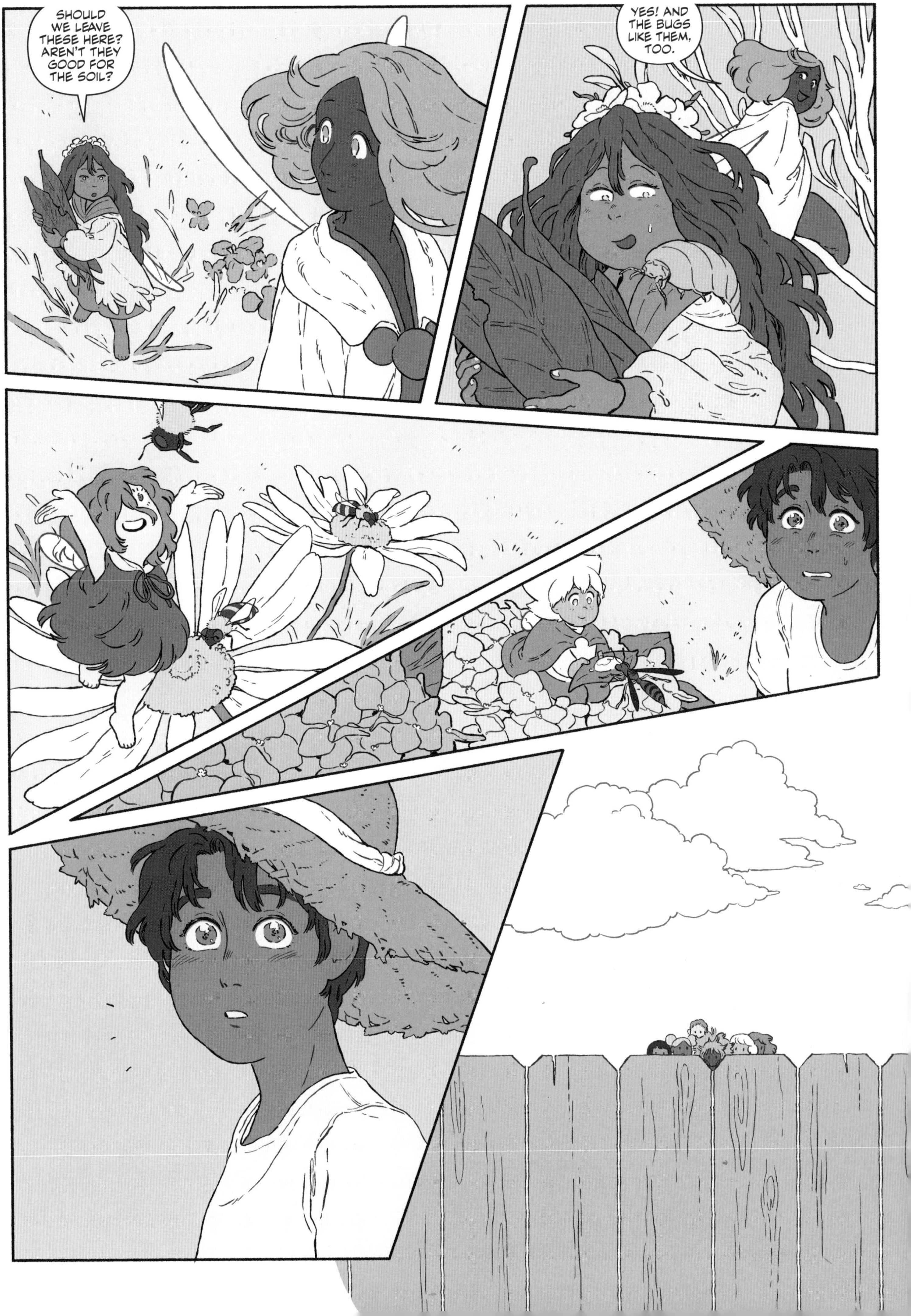
SHOULD WE LEAVE THESE HERE? AREN'T THEY GOOD FOR THE SOIL?
YES! AND THE BUGS LIKE THEM, TOO.

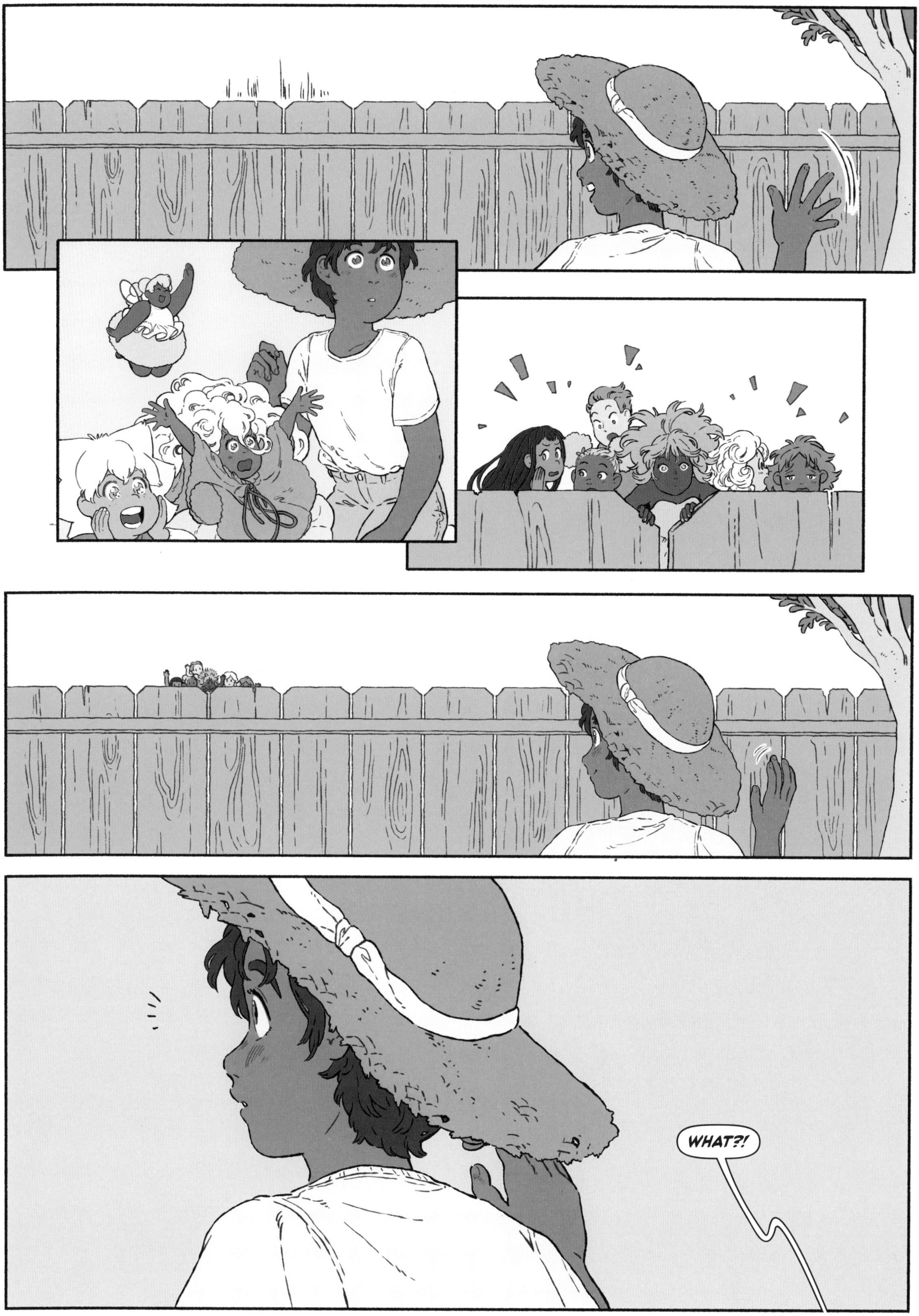
WHAT?!

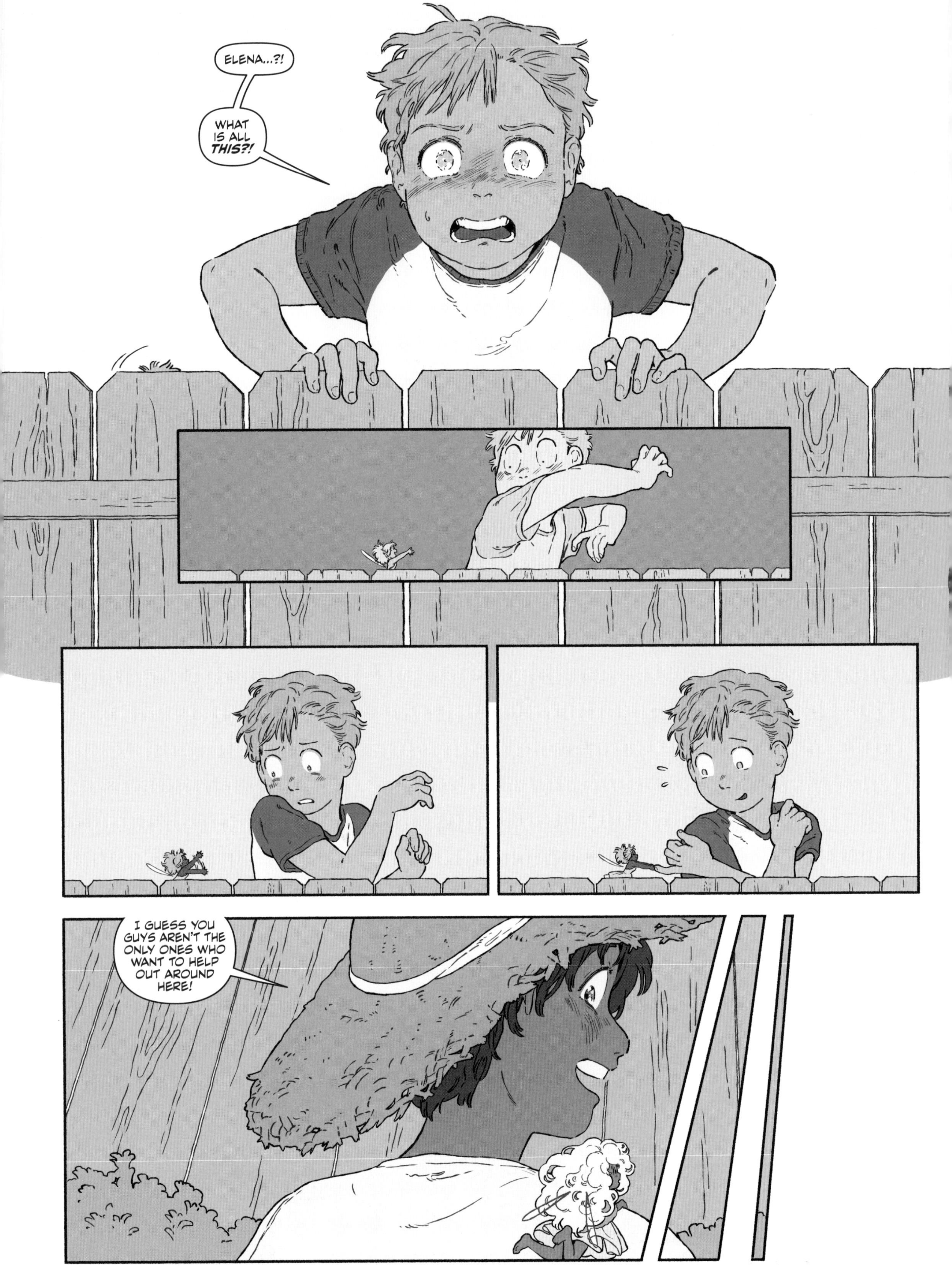
ELENA...?!
WHAT IS ALL THIS?!
I GUESS YOU GUYS AREN'T THE ONLY ONES WHO WANT TO HELP OUT AROUND HERE!

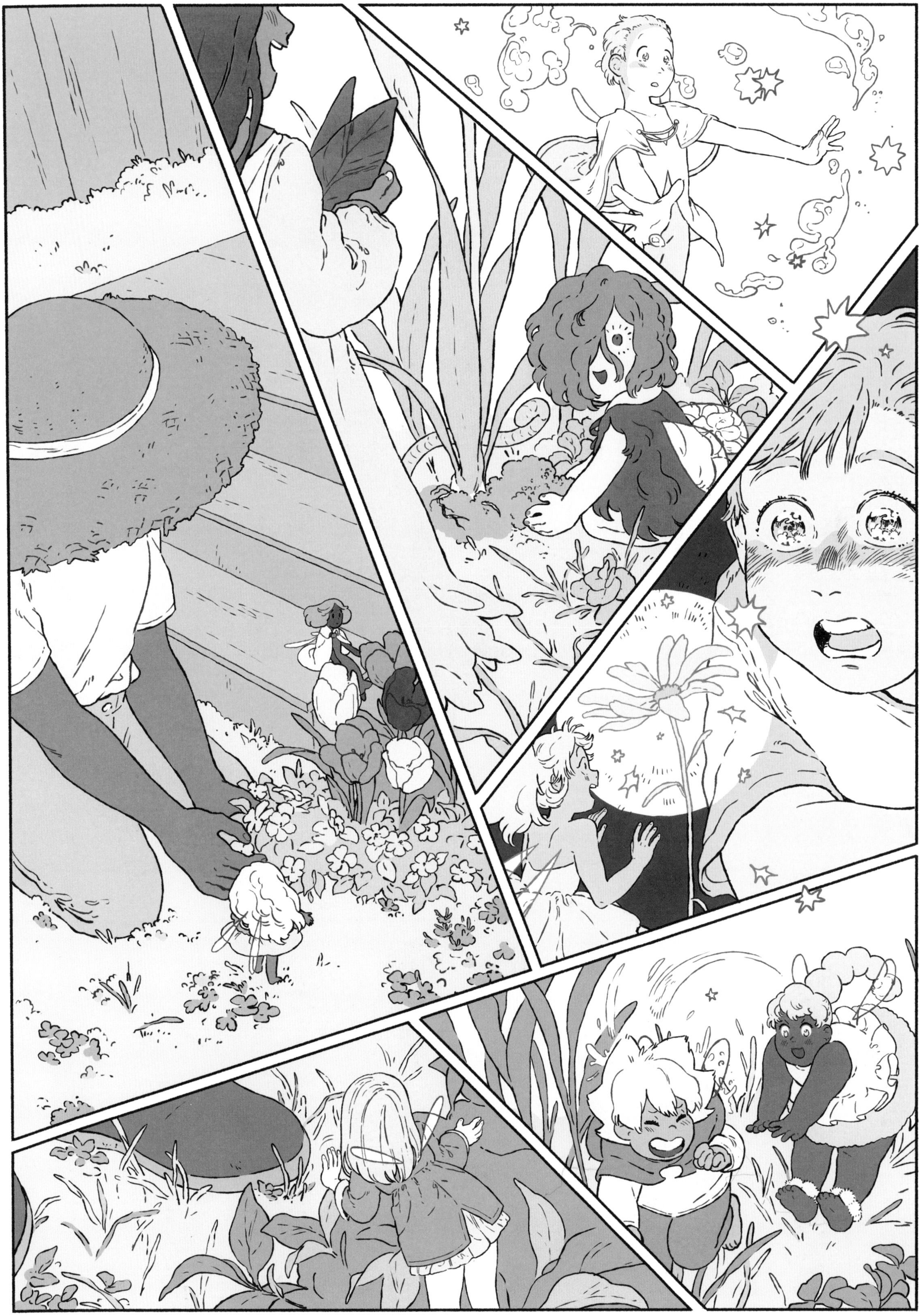

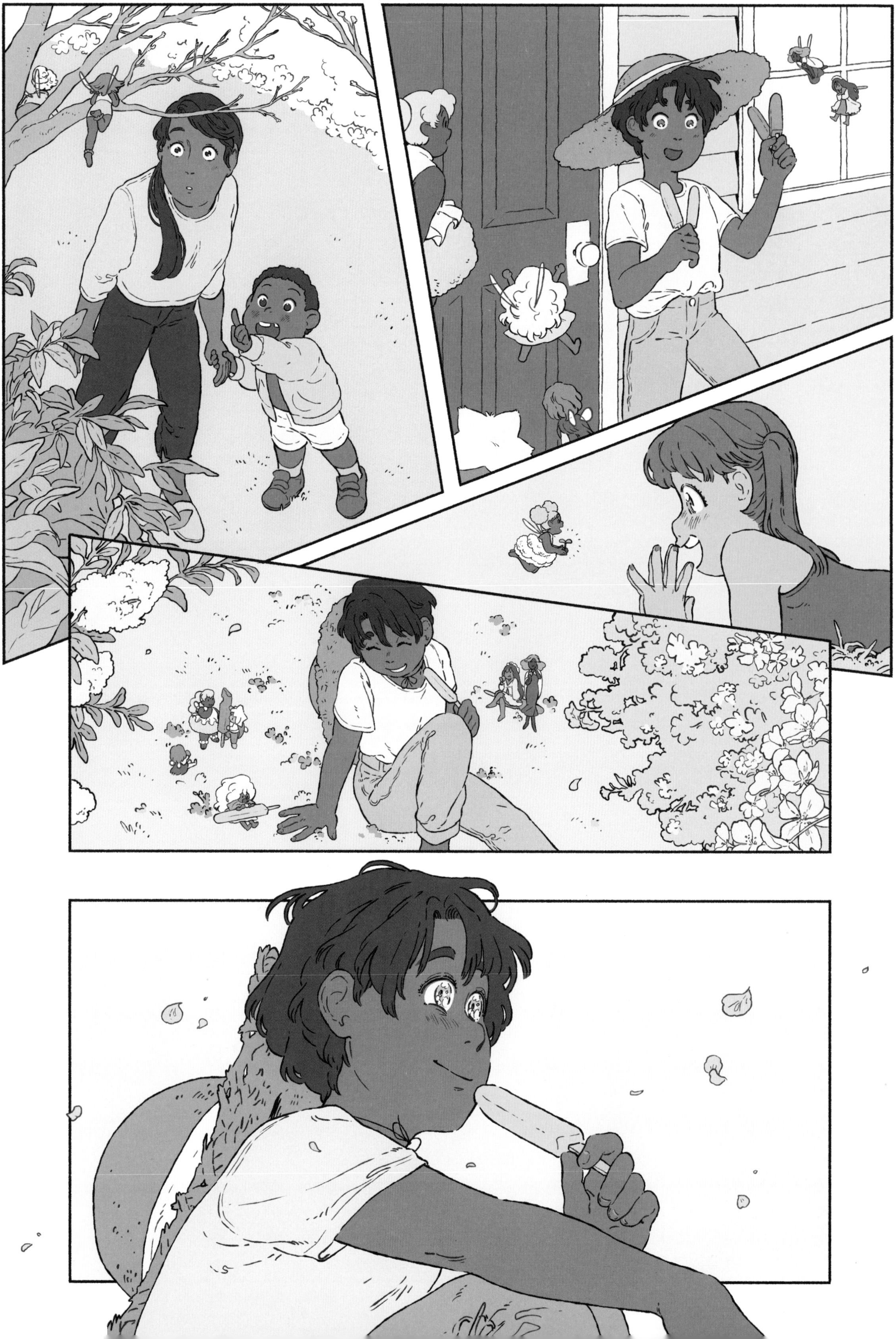

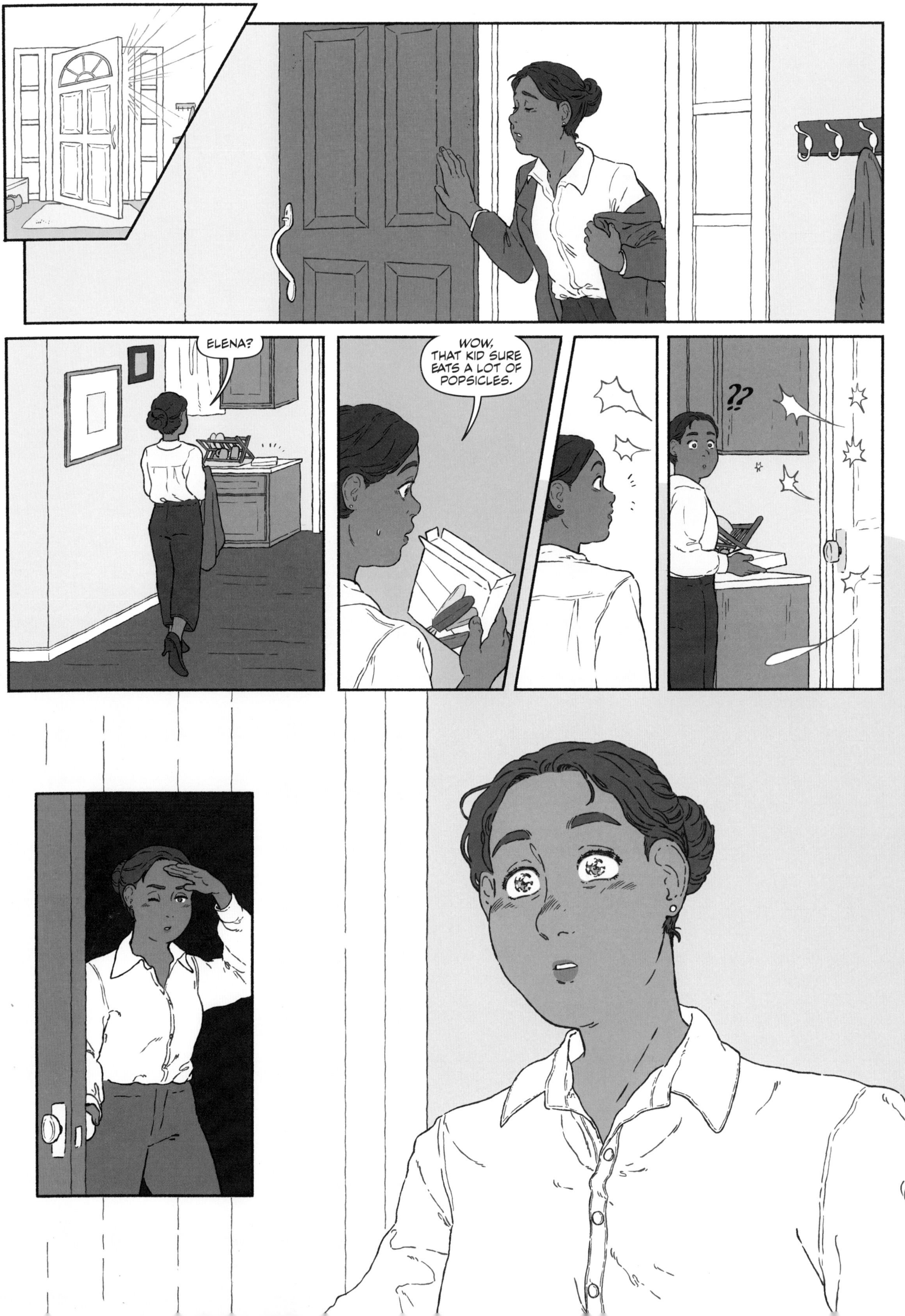
ELENA?
WOW, THAT KID SURE EATS A LOT OF POPSICLES.
??

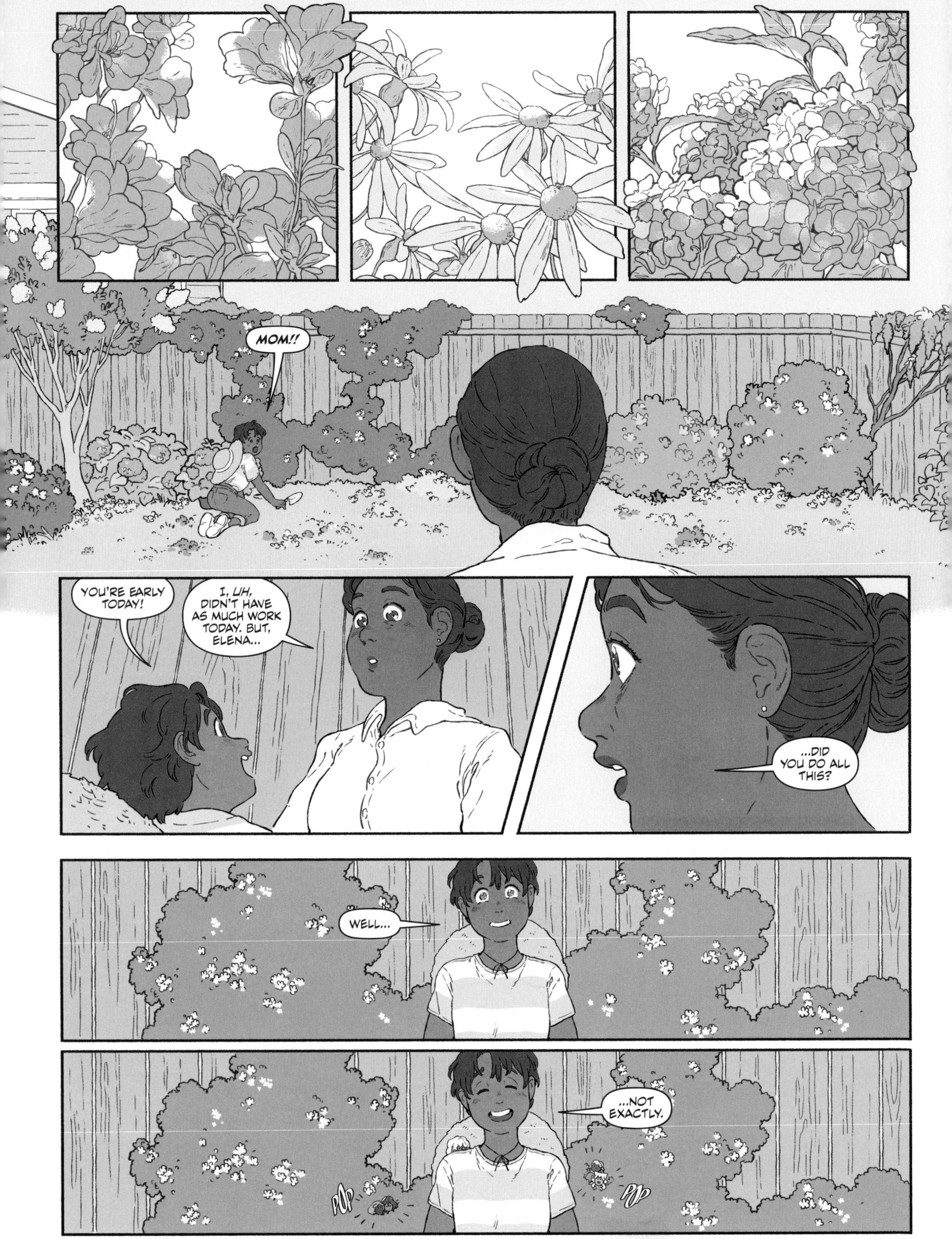
MOM!!
YOU'RE EARLY TODAY!
I, *UH*, DIDN'T HAVE AS MUCH WORK TODAY. BUT, ELENA...
...DID YOU DO ALL THIS?
WELL...
...NOT EXACTLY.
POP
POP

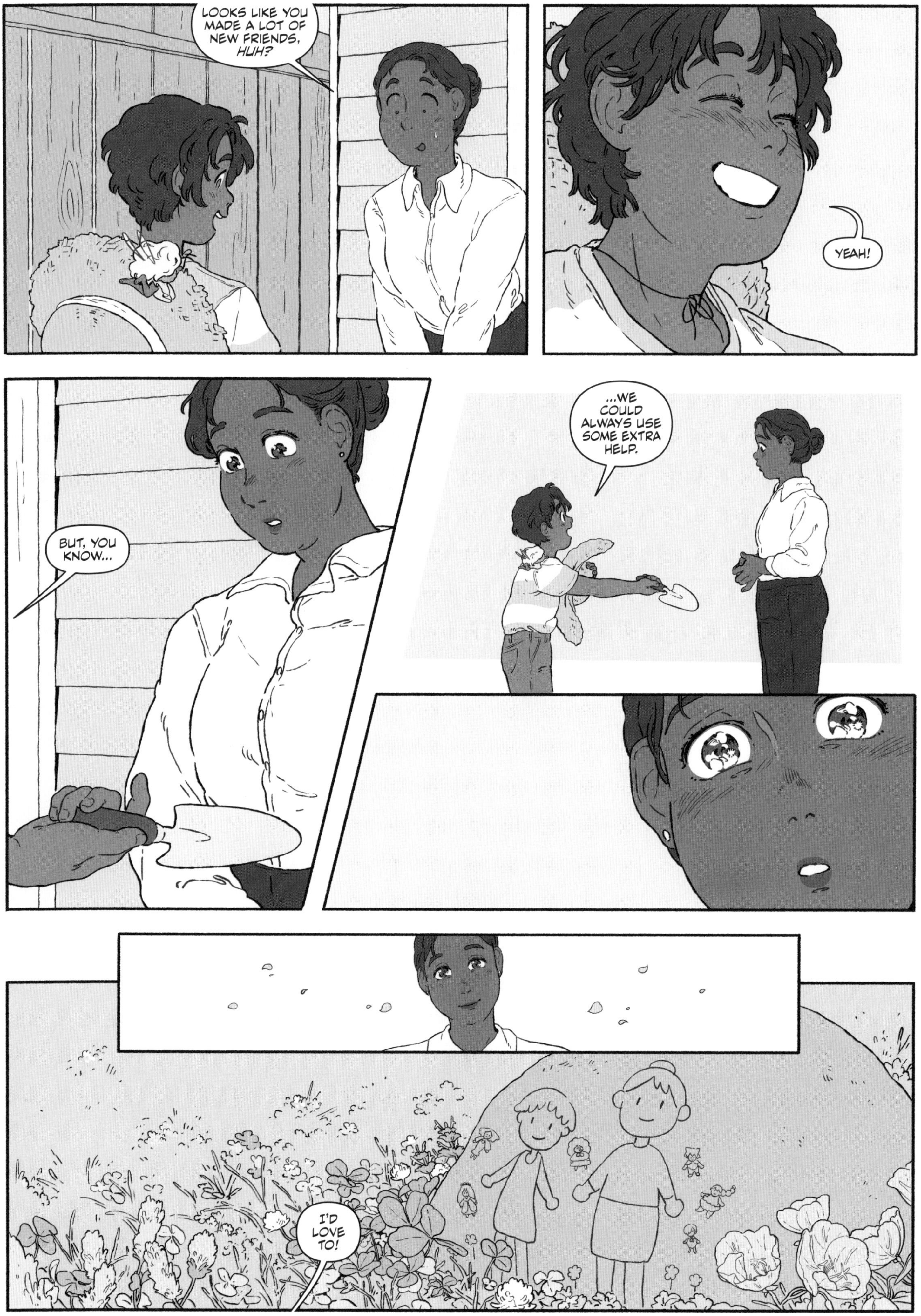
LOOKS LIKE YOU MADE A LOT OF NEW FRIENDS, *HUH?*
YEAH!
BUT, YOU KNOW...
...WE COULD ALWAYS USE SOME EXTRA HELP.
I'D LOVE TO!

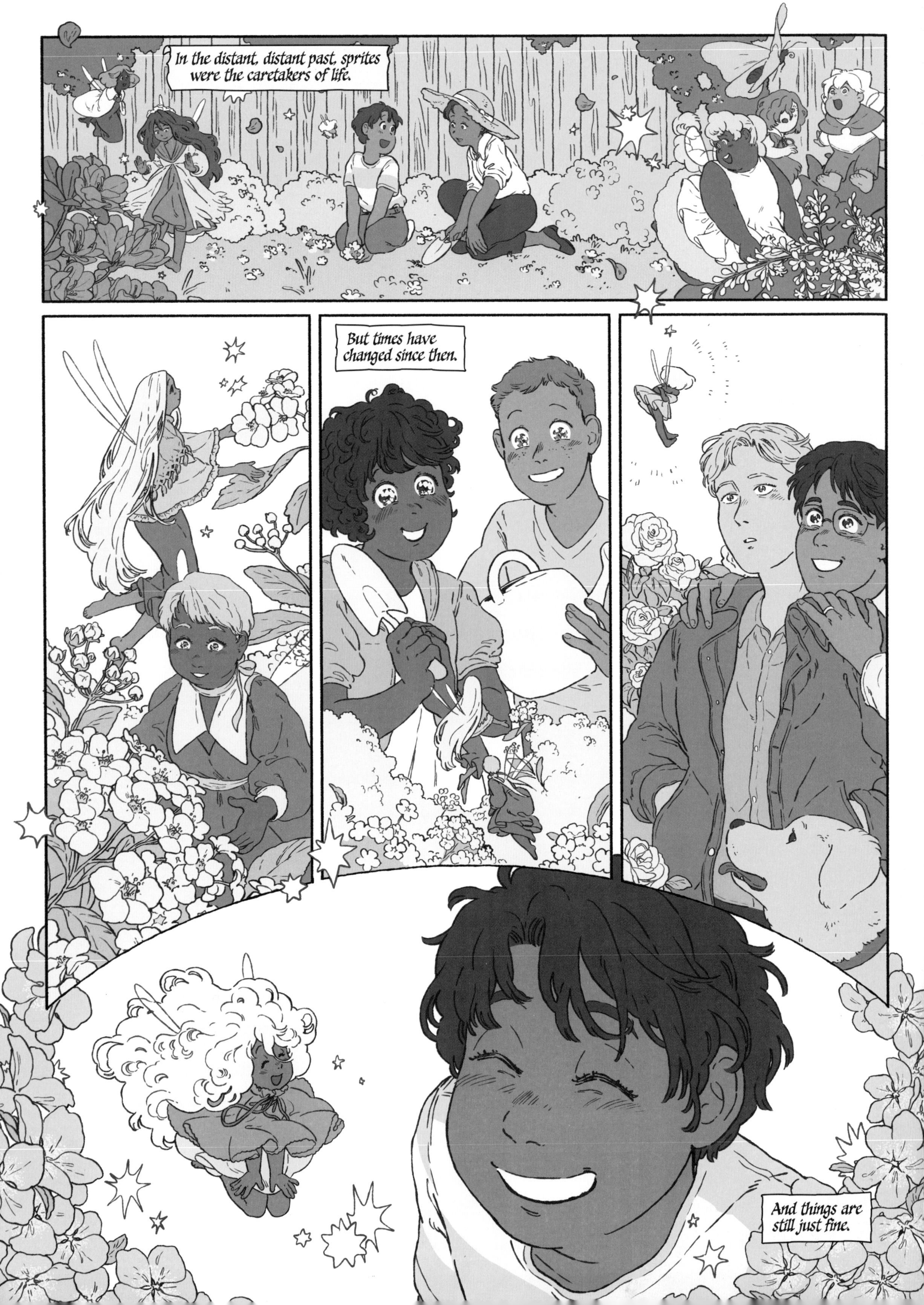
In the distant, distant past, sprites were the caretakers of life.
But times have changed since then.
And things are still just fine.

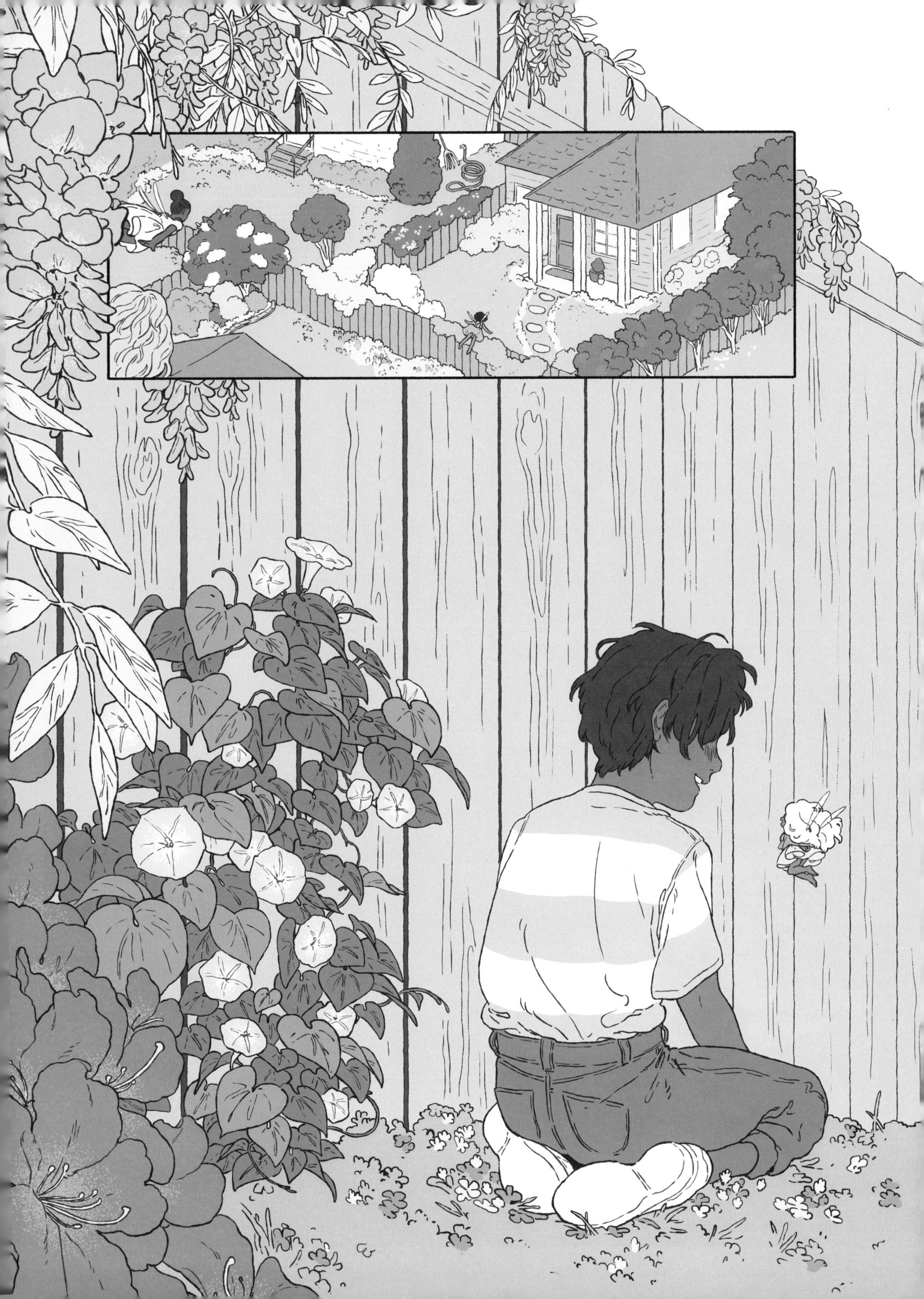

In fact, they're better than ever.

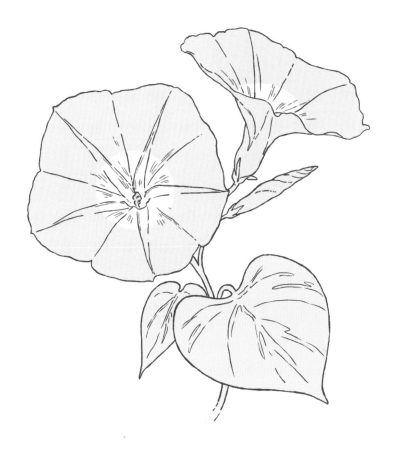

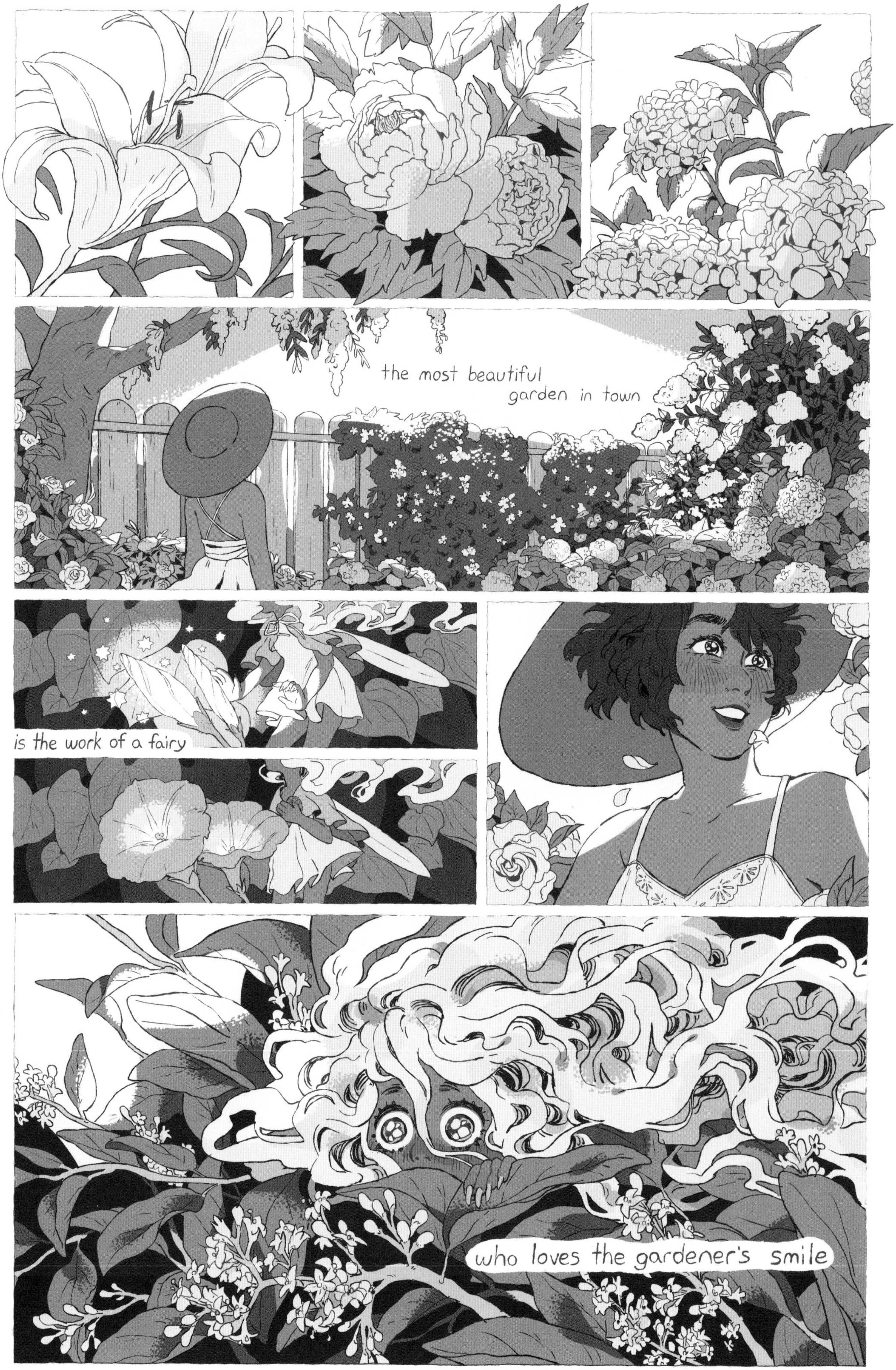
the most beautiful
garden in town
is the work of a fairy
who loves the gardener's smile

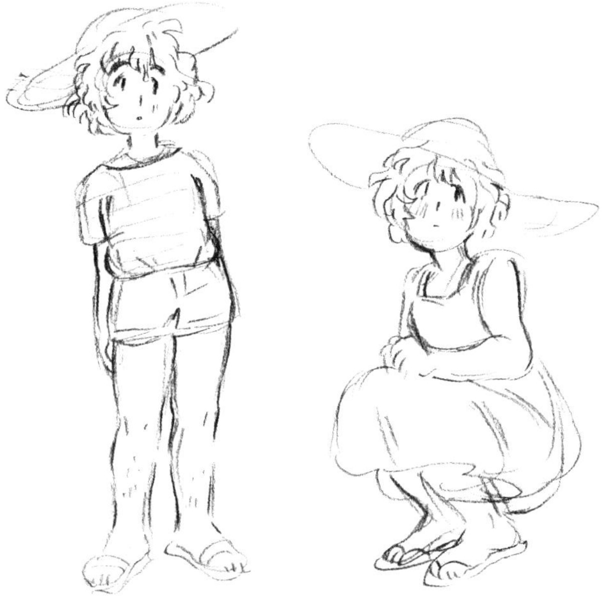

Making of *The Sprite and the Gardener*

The Sprite and the Gardener had small beginnings—it was initially conceived of as a single self-contained page by Rii Abrego. It later became a collaborative project co-written by Joe Whitt, who also helped lay the groundwork for additional character designs and some early page layouts.

The following pages feature art by both Rii and Joe.

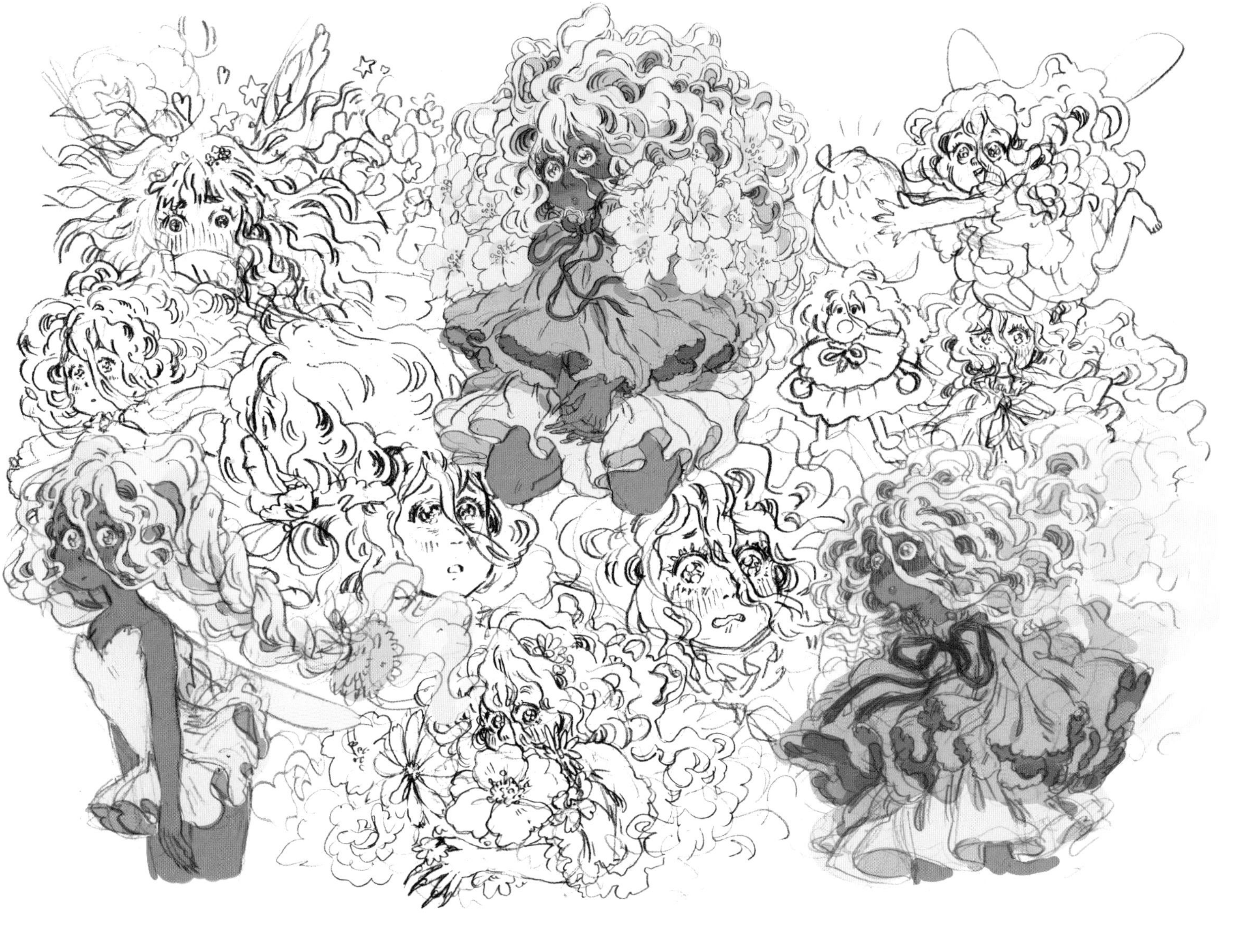

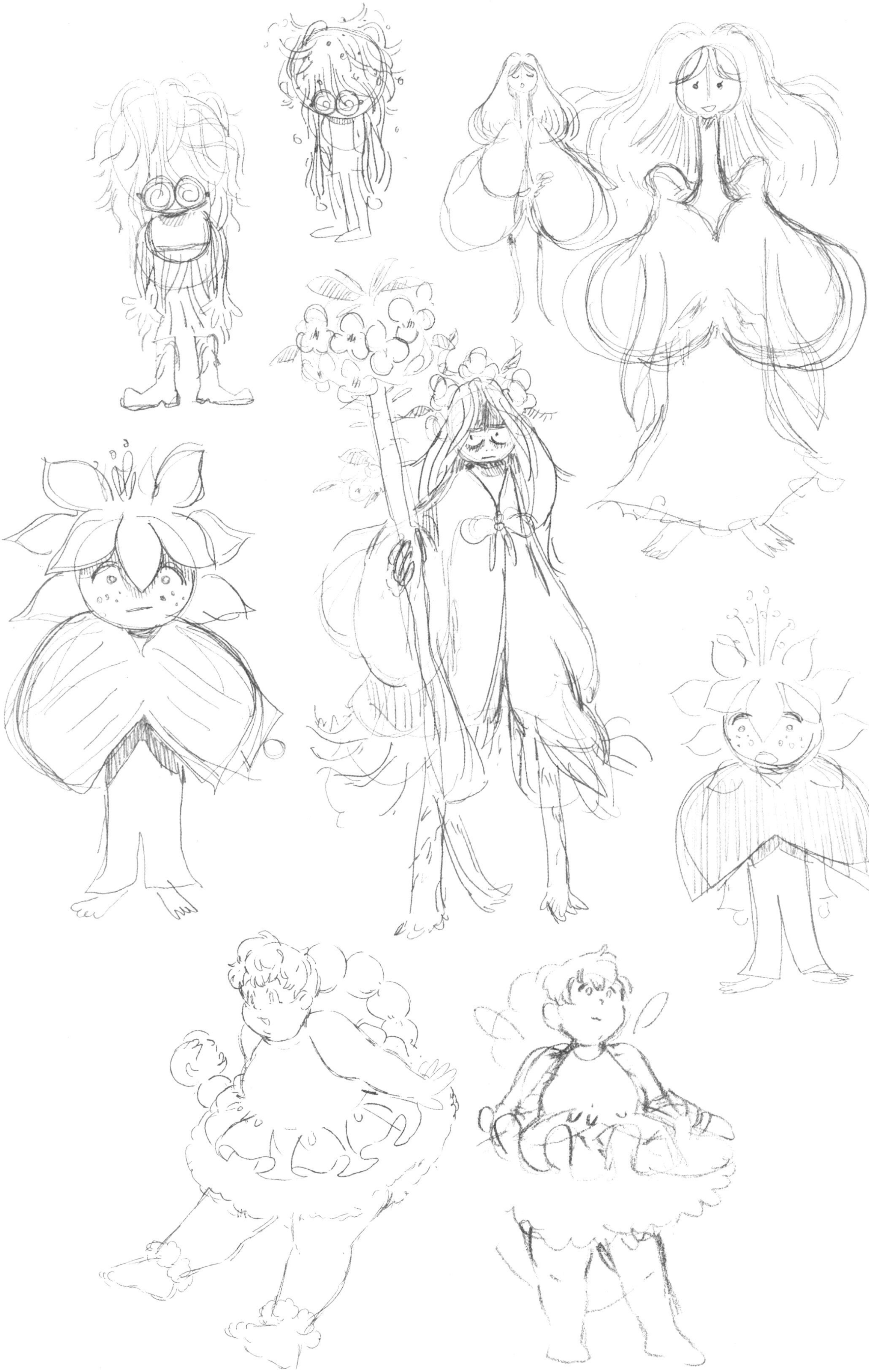

Rii Abrego

is a Latina illustrator who resides in the very green, very humid southern USA. She is an admirer of big bugs and a magnet for stray cats. *The Sprite and the Gardener* is her debut original graphic novel.

Thank you to Ari, who gave us our starting point, and to Grace, Robin, Sarah, Crank, and everyone else at Oni Press who helped us clear the finish line. Thank you to my parents, whose tireless faith in my shaky drawings of anime girls helped me hold on to dreams that were born decades ago. And thank you to Joe, my friends, my peers, and anyone who has cheered me on from the sidelines—I don't know where I would be without your enduring support. —Rii

Joe Whitt

is a comic artist based in Alabama. He graduated from the University of Montevallo with a BFA in drawing. He lives with three polite cats. This is his graphic novel debut.

Thanks to Ari, Sarah, Robin, and Grace for all their exceptional editorship and for helping us give this book some legs, and to Crank for the wonderful lettering job. Thanks to Mom and Dad for their support and for never telling me to stop drawing, even though I was pretty bad at it. Thanks to the public libraries of Jefferson County for all the manga I've borrowed, to Mr. Griffin for expecting things of me, and to Rii for asking me to be a part of this and for drawing such a good-looking book. —Joe

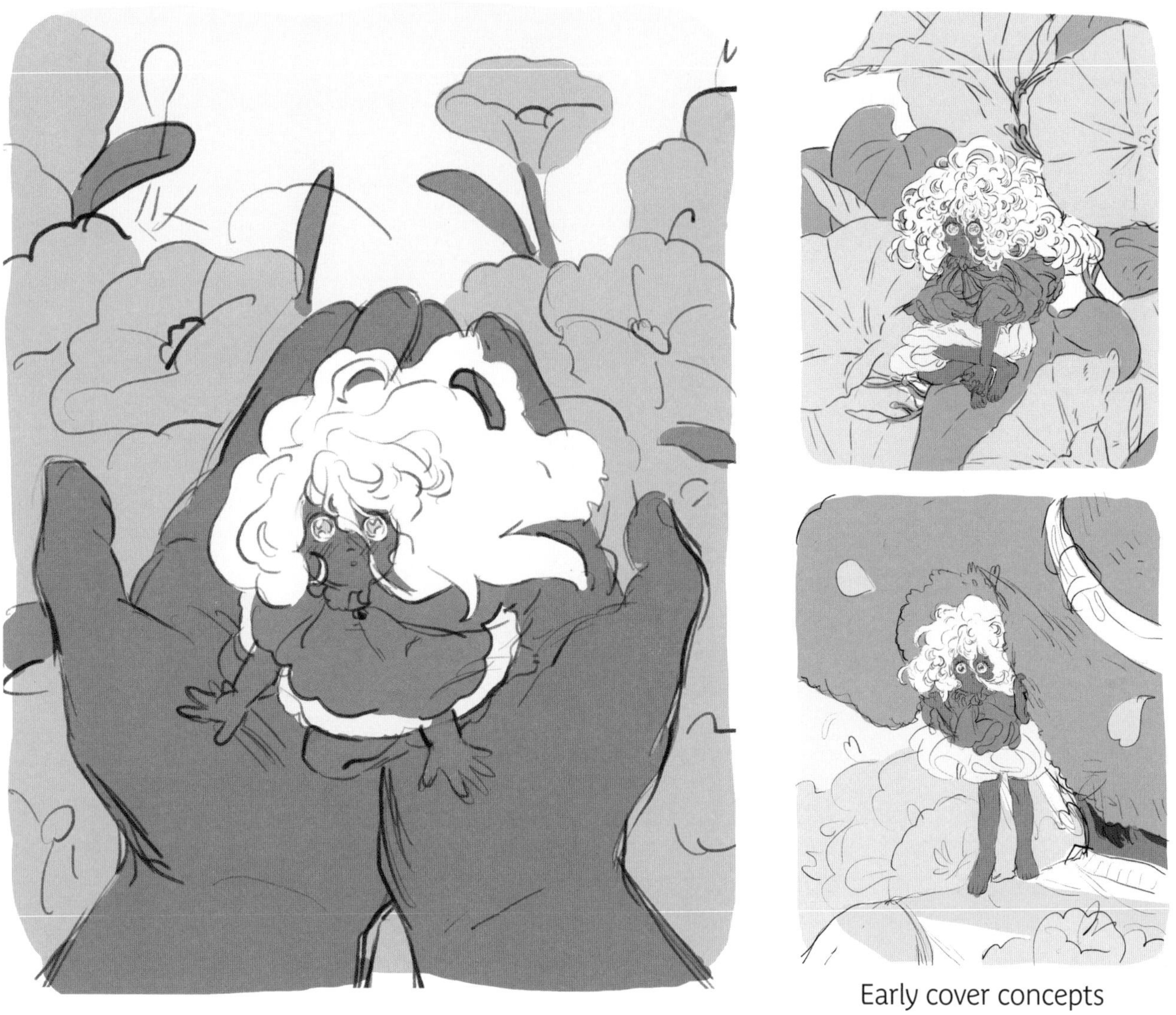

Early cover concepts

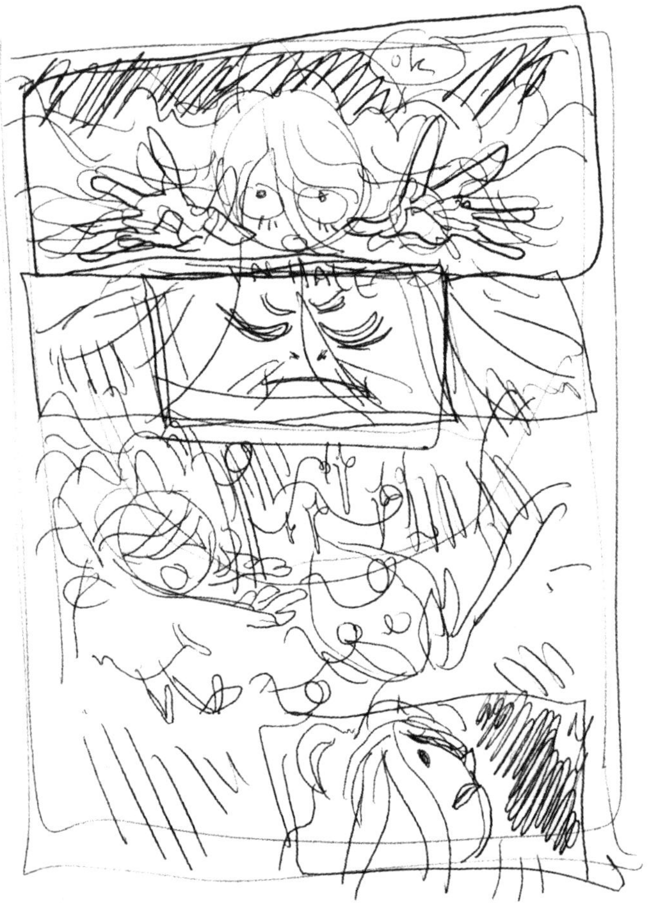

Joe's initial thumbnail

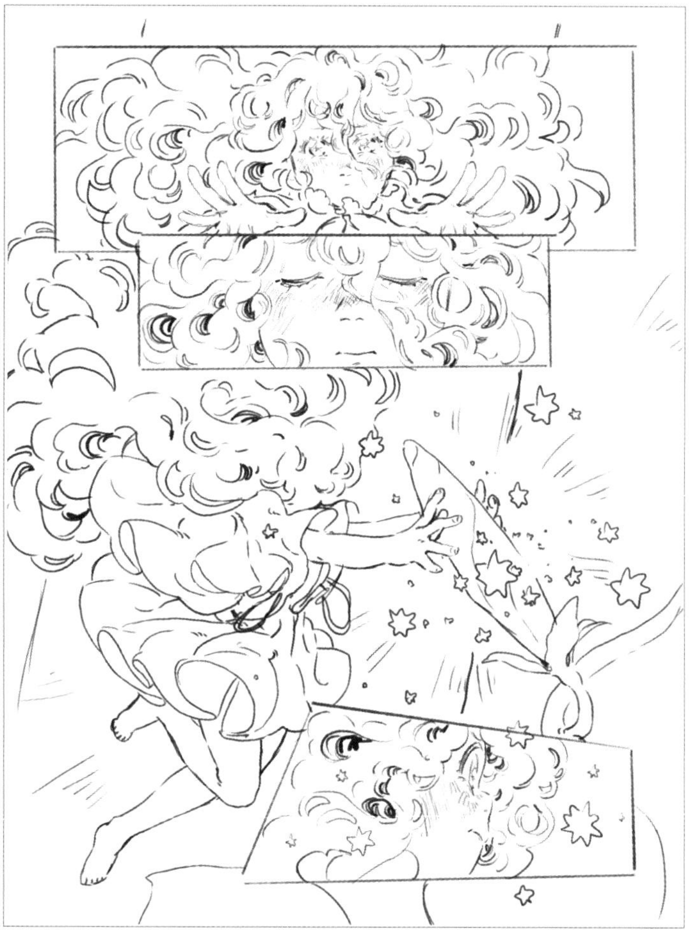

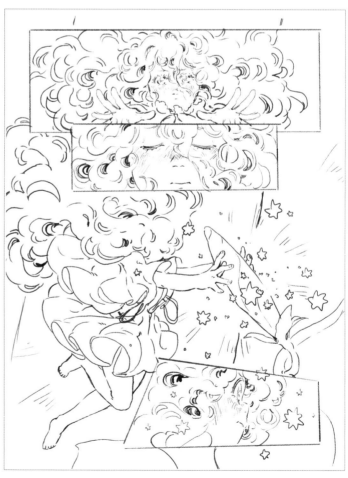

Rii's final sketch